BLACK
SNOW
FALLING

L.J. MacWhirter

Scotland Street Press

Published by Scotland Street Press 2018

Copyright © 2018 L.J. MacWhirter
All rights reserved.

L. J. MacWhirter acknowledges support from Creative
Scotland towards the writing of this book.

A CIP catalogue reference for this book is available from the British Library.

First published in Scotland in 2018 by
Scotland Street Press
scotlandstreetpress@gmail.com

ISBN: 978-1-910895-21-4

Typeset by Hewer Text UK Ltd, Edinburgh
Printed in Poland

Cover design by Tim Byrne

L.J. MacWhirter was born just outside London and grew up in the North of England. After studying English Literature, she went on to become an award-winning creative copywriter. *Black Snow Falling* is her debut novel. She lives in Edinburgh with her family.

To my daughter
Jenny

We are such stuff
As dreams are made on, and our little life
Is rounded with a sleep

William Shakespeare

Nothing is so uncertain or less enduring than the life of
man, who truly . . . is nothing less than a dream of
shadows

Princess Elizabeth (later Queen Elizabeth I)

Time slips between 1543, 1592 and some unearthly place . . .

1543 – The Sleeping Lad

Moonlight poured through the attic window above the candle-maker's shop. Slumped asleep over a desk was a boy. His name was Jude. Scribbled notes were strewn all around him and his wax-splattered apron was cast aside on a straw mattress. As he breathed, a blanket slipped from his shoulders, exposing the cobbled line of his spine and bruises dark as plums. The rest of his skin was ghostly white in the half-light. His shoulder blades rose and fell with the pace of deep sleep. Shadows curved along his young muscles. Lank hair fell across his face. Even asleep, his jaw jutted forwards a little.

Jude was resting on his work. The candle on the desk – one of his father's rejects – had long since burnt to its base, and he still held the feather quill which touched the last words he had written, *heavenly orbs*. Ink bloomed in the *s* and spidered across the page.

He stirred once again and his breathing steadied. Moonlight trembled as if a cloud had passed through its beam. Except it wasn't a cloud.

A creature so tall it had to stoop beneath the rafters was watching him sleep. Its body, face, arms and legs burned with a smoky black fire, yet its flames burned silently and the claws on its feet left no tracks in the dust on the floor.

Up it crept to the lone boy. It seemed to be drawn by a light shining around Jude's head, a spinning halo of iridescent colours, rings of gold, cherry red, the brightest emerald and deepest indigo. His dream. Faster and faster these bands of colour whirled until they blurred together into pure white light. This shining dreamlight stretched across Jude's face as if caressing his cheeks and hair and beyond, illuminating the pile of notes and the boxes of rejected candles stacked all around.

The creature saw that the humble attic above a tradesman's shop was a place of study, and its black eyes shot back greedily to the boy's dream, one of those powerful ones spurring him to aspire beyond his station in life. As the dream shone at its strongest, the creature moved closer.

Deftly, it extended one finger and with its razor-sharp nail scored a line all the way around the inside of the spinning halo: the first separation of the dream from the dreamer. The halo singed and burned red-hot, blackening to charcoal. The creature dipped its dark flame hand in further still, its tongue flickering over its lips as it pulled at the blackening dream. Jude's head lifted from the desk and his sleeping body arced in the air as his soul tried to hold onto his dream. But it was impossible. The invisible sinews, so deeply attaching the boy to his dream, were stretched, stretched, and severed. His body fell back onto the desk. His dream had been ripped away.

The dream thief hooped the darkened dream halo over its arm, up alongside the other dreams it had stolen that night, and watched, smirking, as tears began rolling down Jude's cheeks and across his notes. The boy's words bled and dissolved in the tears.

2

1592 – A Haunting Dream

Ice crystals flew up from Ruth's skates as she powered across the frozen lake, hair flying out behind her. Meg gasped and flagged behind. Ruth whirled around, laughing, as Meg grimaced, wobbling on her skates. She felt Silas's eyes upon her and looked beyond Meg to the edge of the wood where he was standing between the two horses – but he glanced away as the Steward passed by. The man was stalking up and down beside the coach, banging his gloved hands together in the cold. All were dark figures against the white snow, still bright in the falling light, cloaking the trees against a sky growing fierce beyond.

Silas turned, his dark hair and coat swinging to one side as he rounded the horse to the left and stroked its neck with long, firm sweeps. Those hands. She could almost feel them on her hair, on her cheek, or holding the small of her back.

He sat down on a fallen branch, reached for a stone and took out his hunting knife to sharpen. She longed for more time alone with him. She knew he felt the same. Over Christmas there had been even fewer chances for their secret meetings.

Her eyes flicked back to Meg, who was finding her stride and coming closer. Meg gave her a knowing smile; Silas was no secret between them. The smile turned into a frown as Meg swayed from side to side, her skates thudding on the ice – her friend was more comfortable with a needle in her hand than blades on her feet. Ruth checked for her little globe, safe in her pocket, waiting until the last moment with the toe of her skate pressed into the ice, and sprang away just as Meg's hand reached for her arm. Meg cried out in frustration. And as Ruth swung around in triumph, out of the corner of her eye she saw, falling from her pocket, her precious little globe. It bounced, bounced and skittered across the lake.

"No!" She'd never forgive herself if she lost it!

Ruth chased after the miniature globe as it raced away . . . as though it too was part of the game. Over and over it rolled, all the painted countries and seas of the Earth lost in a spinning blur. *It was your Grandfather Richard's most treasured Curiosity* . . . her long-dead mother's words echoed in her mind. To lose their favourite thing would be unbearable. It skidded towards the edge of the lake. The rocks! It would smash into a thousand pieces. Ruth dived onto the ice to save it, hands outstretched. Geese panicked and flew up squawking as she slid on the ice and grabbed it just in time.

Catching her breath, she gathered herself upright, flicked her long hair out of her eyes and slowly opened her hand, red and grazed from the rough landing. She rolled the globe around her palm with one finger, inspecting the damage. The paint was chipped. She bit her lip. Despite layers of varnish, Spain had lost swathes of land. It was all but gone. Their old enemy, obliterated – were that really so easy, it would no doubt please the Queen.

A memory flashed from long ago. Ruth being swung up high by her mother and hugged tight as she pressed her nose against the glass of their Cabinet of Curiosities, gazing at the treasures inside. They had a little ritual. Ruth would point and her mother would tell the familiar old story . . . where the Curiosity was found and by whom, and how it was passed down the years from great-grandfather, to Grandfather Richard and then to his daughter, her mother. Of all the Curiosities, the little pocket globe fascinated her the most, its enchanting inky-blue-gold loveliness tempting her to touch it.

These days there was no-one to stop her taking whatever she wanted from the cabinet – her father was away so often, trading on the silk route. She traced his path on the globe with her fingertip. In his absence, the key to the cabinet belonged to her. Her hand trembled as she enclosed the globe in her palm, a drop of blood oozing from the graze and falling onto the ice. She winced.

"'Tis safe?" Meg asked, out of breath, as she finally caught up. Ruth shook ice and snow off her cape.

Black snow.

That dream again! It flitted across her mind like a haunting. Ever since the dream had come to her over a week ago, it had barely left. It made her feel so uneasy.

"Ruth?"

"Yes, it's safe." She opened her palm to reveal it.

"Thank goodness. Charming little thing."

As Meg fiddled with her skates, Ruth thought to check the golden chain, dangling it carefully, then the tiny clasp. It was bent. She pushed it open with her fingernail. The two halves fell open as they should, jointed together, revealing the two domes of the night sky with golden stars. They looked perfect. Perfect and innocent. Like the vast old Armillary Sphere in the Hall's library, which showed the Moon and stars obediently turning around Earth at the centre of the heavens. It didn't betray the remotest hint of those dangerous rumours that so intrigued her, those Copernican heresies that stood conventional thinking on its head and sent the Royal Court and Rome spinning into condemnation fifty years ago.

She glanced up at the sky. The clouds were thick and scudding. The stars, those contentious fiery orbs, would be keeping their counsel tonight. Soon it would be starless, moonless. Pitch black.

Black snow, swirling.

That dream again!

"Ruth . . . Ruth!" Meg was saying. "You *are* distracted today. Your Steward!"

The Steward was shouting across the lake, motioning to leave. Ruth climbed to her feet. The wind was building, though she was sure the Steward relished cutting short their time. It was always obvious that he did not like her. He had arrived at Crowbury Hall as part of her stepmother's household – and that was enough for him to be set against her, such was her relationship with the Countess.

Ruth was determined to skate in the opposite direction for one last turn, but as she stepped out, Meg stopped her, gripping her arm. She was blinking rapidly, struggling to get her words out.

"Dear Ruth . . . dear thing, there's something I must tell you."

3

Fifty Years Before . . . Lost Words

Jude rubbed his temples, screwing up his face. He was waiting outside the banqueting chamber at Crowbury Hall, his hand on the colossal new Armillary Sphere that he was about to present. It was so vast it dwarfed him. Even through the door, the music, the chatter and clinking of glasses were deafening. His heart pounded so fast that his tunic trembled. Since he'd woken, none of the speech he'd prepared would come back to him. Words had vanished from his head overnight like seeds washed away by rain. He was about to address hundreds of guests *and* King Henry! They would think him an idiot, a laughing stock.

All day long, in between making candles, he had frantically tried to memorise his notes once again. But every word he stamped on his brain fell off; the boy he was yesterday seemed out of reach. What had happened to him?

His head swivelled, looking around anxiously for Richard, the Earl of Crowbury's son, who had helped him write the speech. Richard would help him remember! Quickly, Jude searched along the corridor and checked the staircase, but there was no sign of him. By now Richard would usually have come to greet him and make sure all was well. So where was he? Why hadn't he come, as he'd promised?

Jude returned to the Armillary Sphere and steadied his hand on the solid brass. Under his sweaty touch it was smooth and cold. It glowed in a sudden burst of light from a spitting torch on the wall. The same light showed up his Master Curiosity clothes, clean an hour ago but now splattered with mud. Jude dabbed at the spots and cursed the weather. Why did the heavens have to open and bear down upon him just as he'd sprinted up the lane?

He pulled out his sodden notes from his pocket. The wet pages would not separate – the storm had blurred all the ink, after the words on the cover had mysteriously run during the night. He shoved the papers back. They were useless. Even reading the speech aloud would be impossible.

Moments tick-tocked past. Just a few more and he would be called into the chamber. Above the sounds of the feast, a burst of raucous laughter came from inside – unmistakably the King's. No-one else would dare to be so loud.

An oboe's sinuous tune reached Jude. Closing his eyes, he tried to recall their conversations as they'd written the speech. He muttered random fragments. What was it Richard had stressed? It was crucial he get this right. Yes, that was it! Jude absolutely *should* – or was it absolutely *should not*? – mention that clever new book . . . *On the Revolution of . . .* what was the rest of its title? Those revolutionary ideas . . . did Richard say they would impress or disturb the King? Jude pushed his thumbs into his temples. But the King was famous for welcoming radical things. He was an enlightened modern man. He'd even divorced England from Rome, founding his own Church of England and appointing himself as its head. Would he not welcome another notion that turned convention upside down?

Jude's thoughts rattled and jarred. Snippets of the speech surfaced – only to be snatched away once again. His eyes felt wet. He rubbed them dry on the back of his sleeve.

Two passing maidservants clucked their disapproval. He shrank into his clothes.

This was not the first time Richard had invited him to present the family's latest curiosities at a feast. He took a breath. But though nerves had sometimes troubled him, he'd never before forgotten his words. Not for the split stones with ghostly imprints of leaves and coiled shells, nor the ancient Royal Inca drinking cup, nor the new little painted pocket globe with its gold chain and gold-leaf stars inside, of which Richard was so fond. Jude's introductions had not been artful but all had been well. And he'd been liked.

Inside the chamber, the musicians played on. Not long now.

Gathering himself, Jude took in the interlocking circles and globes of the Armillary Sphere, this heavy representation of the heavens. He reached inside and felt the cold brass of the moving stars, the crystal white Moon, the pale yellow marble Sun. Leaning in, his hand could only reach halfway around the largest globe in the centre: Earth . . . in the very heart of the heavens, as most folk believed, save for that ingenious writer – what *was* his name? Jude felt the Earth's mass in his hand. He traced the ragged lines of the New World, moved back over to the Old World, found England under his fingertip and pressed in his nail, willing it to speak the answer.

He'd had only a few days to acquaint himself with the Armillary Sphere, but a whole month in the company of that radical book.

Each night, when his father finally released him from the candle workshop, he would dash upstairs to his attic room. There, he would sit under the stars shining through his little window and dutifully guide his quill, copying the shape of each Latin letter on every page. Richard had said that another copy of the book would be useful. Not that Jude understood the Latin text – Richard had explained it all to him. Like paper taking ink, Jude thirstily absorbed the fascinating message . . . it turned the heavens upside down . . . but what *was* it again? This evening he just couldn't remember anything. Jude rubbed the aching bruises on his arm. Copying the letters and diagrams was also a distraction from his father's fists. That man beat the life out of him. Yet hope always used to spring back, helped by working with Richard in his library. It was a world away from the cruelty at home. Seeing the Earl's Collection of Curiosities used to help, too. These strange objects came from another world beyond his imagination.

"Few have seen such a wondrous mechanical object," Richard had said of the Armillary Sphere when it arrived at Crowbury Hall the previous week. "They will be captivated by what you show them. All eyes will be on you – trust me!"

Only yesterday Jude had dared to believe he'd be capable of making a presentation that would do justice to it.

Tonight, he knew, would be an altogether different story.

He hoped his audience would be distracted by the sphere's mechanical turning and barely notice his stumbling performance. His face reddened, dreading what would come next. Without a sensible thought in his head – without Richard – Jude's guts had turned to molten wax . . . his legs, guttering stumps on the verge of collapse.

4

A Snatched Moment

Ruth drummed her fingers on the coach windowsill, her mind full of Meg. They headed homewards, wheels skidding over ice. As they clattered over the bridge into Crowbury, her skates fell off the seat beside her. Wind whistled around the coach's loose wooden frame. Ruth shivered, tucked the blanket around her legs and aching ankles, and drew her cape tight. More snowflakes flew past. It was so cold that ice had crept in even further from the edge of the fields, crystallising the reeds, stilling the river apart from a few ripples that ran down the middle where the wind caught the surface. A heavy grey fog was gathering. It rolled upriver from where the Thames was wider in London to these meandering upper reaches.

For once, Crowbury's ramshackle buildings and raggle-taggle market square looked almost pretty, iced with snow in the dusk. Through her window she watched a blur of activity. Tradesmen hefted crates and rumbled past with carts, rushing to close up their stalls and shops before the coming storm. Once, her father had pointed out how hard the townsfolk worked behind these quiet-looking exteriors ... all the forging, the cobbling, the baking, the stitching and embroidering. A butcher, frowning, carried half a pig over his shoulder, unsold.

Close by, a shutter banged. Ruth jumped. She turned. It was the candle-maker's. Something about the place made her shudder. A memory. An entry in grandfather's journal about a candle-maker, a vicious man who once lived here with his son.

She strains to see through the storm of falling shadows.

Ruth took a deep breath and shook her head – that dream again. Always needling her. Always at the edge of her sight.

One or two men she half-recognised from the Christmas feast the night before, tipped their caps at her window. She hardly noticed them as she rubbed her tired eyes. The whole evening had felt a little strange. Her stepmother had been colder towards her than usual, making her father's absence even harder to bear. He had been away for almost a year. She had given no welcoming speech to the townsfolk and had given out no parcels to the sick. All her promises to care for Crowbury in her husband's absence had turned out to be empty. Yet the feast had gone well; folk were undaunted, thankful for a better year. 1592 had been kinder than people had feared, with fuller bellies and fewer deaths. The harvest had been saved before the storms. Mercifully, the plague had been confined to London.

But even after the celebrations, that dream had come to her.

The coach racked and bumped. From the driver's seats upfront, the Steward shouted and cracked the whip. Too many times. Beside him, Silas would no doubt be wincing, but would say nothing.

Cold numbed her fingers. She rubbed them together and blew into her cupped palms. Trees creaked and swayed as the wind gusted, sending snow clumping to the ground, exposing branches and trunks, wet and dark. Fresh snowflakes tumbled across her view.

They drew level with the graveyard. Winter made it look more ghoulish than ever. Clods of frozen earth were piled up beside a fieldstone. A fresh grave. Glimpsing the church beyond, Ruth twisted the cape between her fingers. Her mother was lying there, at peace. Her chest tightened. She yearned to tell her what Meg had said – she could barely take it in. Meg had dreaded telling her, practically mumbling the words into Ruth's sleeve on the ice.

So Meg was to marry. At fifteen. It still did not quite feel true. "A daughter's duty," Meg had said.

Ruth said a few sharp words, which she now regretted. They had travelled the rest of the way back to Meg's house in silence and dropped her off without their usual farewells. Why had Ruth felt so angry? She wasn't sure. She would miss her terribly. Ruth felt a sudden urge to stop the coach and go back. Apologise. Put things right. But it was late, the weather was worsening and she had something else in mind before supper that evening . . . making amends would have to wait. The Steward would never agree to it anyway. She sighed deeply. Her breath fogged the glass so she could no longer see her own dark hair and eyes staring back at her.

The coach rattled along the rest of the way to Crowbury Hall. Meg would move away, Ruth realised, leaving her behind. They'd have no more times together. No more secrets.

Ruth's stepsister Eleanor was the same age as Meg, but they rarely found a civil word for each other, only silence or the occasional jibe or barb. There was none of that with Meg. But marriage would alter her. Meg would have to dress and behave as a married woman, with a lace ruff tied around her neck – so stiff she'd hardly be able to move. Perhaps that was the point. In fact, now she thought of it, they were like the slave neck-collars sketched in her grandfather's journal. She pictured a lace ruff made of iron, weighing heavy on the collarbone, tethered by chains. Marriage. Losing your freedom, being enslaved. She was hardly aware of her own hand coming up to touch her neck.

Then she reached around for her hair and ran her fingers through her locks, briskly twisting them into a knot.

A voice rang out, shouting a greeting. Ruth rubbed a hole in the misted glass to see. It was a girl, shawl-wrapped, carrying a bundle of branches propped in the curve of her waist, walking slowly up the track, avoiding its iced-over puddles. But the greeting had not been for Ruth – the girl's face was turned upwards towards Silas and the Steward. Silas replied; Ruth knew the timbre of his voice, even though she could not hear his words. She suddenly felt uneasy. Though the girl's face was pale with cold, her expression was glowing.

Ruth recognised her now. It was Betsy – that pretty girl whose father had married Silas's aunt. There was only a year or so between the two of them in age.

Silas spoke again – Betsy nodded back and her coy smile grew wide. What had he said?

As the coach drew alongside, Betsy glanced into the carriage. Did her eyes harden as she saw Ruth at the window? Ruth drew back anyway, even though she told herself she shouldn't worry. After all, Silas would consider Betsy as family – a cousin or even a sister. Perhaps that unsettling dream was making Ruth see cause to fear when there was none.

She collected herself as the coach emerged from the wood.

At last they turned through the stone pillars and into the bustling courtyard of Crowbury Hall. The household was still clearing up after the feast. Servants with armfuls of empty platters and cloths tramped through the snow, glancing up at the sky.

Without waiting for the Steward, Ruth opened her own door. Her foot skidded on the slippery ground, sending her colliding with the falconer, Little Luce's father, who righted himself as the hawk on his arm flapped its wings and tore bloody meat from his fist.

"Pardon me, Miss Ruth," the falconer said, grinning and dodging another servant. She smiled and was about to speak when she saw Silas feeding handfuls of hay to the horses. He looked up at her. Her heart leapt. Immediately, his eyes flicked to the falconer and he moved around the beast, out of sight.

"Go into the house now," snapped the Steward, breaking into her thoughts. His tone was always so curt. His dislike of her was perfectly obvious. In fact, since her lessons had stopped over Christmas she felt the Steward's eyes track her every move – like that hawk. He never used to come on her outings to see Meg! What had changed?

Ruth approached the nearest of the horses. She reached out to stroke its mane and ran her hand down the horse's back. Its coat was warm and sweaty. Silas reached over with the brush. His fingertips swept her own in one brief movement as he pulled the brush over the horse's back. She dared to raise her eyes to meet his. He nodded almost imperceptibly. There was such fierce feeling in his eyes. She turned, suppressing a smile. He would have to finish brushing down the horses and tethering them in their stalls, which would take ten minutes or so, and then they would meet up.

She lifted up her skirts, and skidded on the packed snow as she made for the door of the Hall.

5

Master Curiosity

Footsteps echoed down the passageway. Jude's heart lifted, then dropped. No Richard. Instead, the torchlight illuminated two servants carrying empty platters.

Still the words of his speech would not return. Jude's fingers tightened on the Armillary Sphere.

"Oi! Who's that?" said one servant.

Jude started, "It's Master—"

"Ain't that the candle-maker's boy?" said the other.

"Hold your nose – 'e reeks!" They laughed as they walked by.

Jude turned away, digging his fingernails into the palms of his hands. Ridiculed, even while dressed as Master Curiosity! The boys in Crowbury had always taunted and bullied him, saying he stank of dead meat. They were right, he supposed. After all, he spent his days boiling up animal carcasses, skimming off fat to make tallow for his father's candles. And in summer months, rotting carcasses smelt even stronger.

His heart lifted once more as the door to the banqueting chamber swung open. Out spilled light and noise and a bright blur of movement – musicians dressed in animal costumes. No Richard. A bear, rabbit and horse ran by, and a wolf, who snapped his muzzle at Jude.

The courtier inside the chamber nodded at Jude, leaving the door ajar. He would be next, the last on the list for the night's entertainment.

For a moment, he almost took to his heels. Maybe his father was right? Jude was stupid for telling stories of trinkets owned by people with more money than sense, people who had no more care for him than their own stable-boys. But something stopped him from running away. He felt compelled to go through with this and not let Richard down, for this nobleman's son actually believed in him, even if his own father didn't. Their unexpected friendship lifted him out of the pits – and away from his father's punches.

Richard helped people, perhaps out of duty as the heir to his father's title, but he was kind, too. King Henry had been busy sacking the monasteries for their riches, so their handouts to the poor had all but come to an end. It was worse where monasteries were in ruins, as in Crowbury. Even Jude had seen how the wretched had swelled in numbers; the generosity of nobility was never more needed.

Jude had first met Richard in the library, when he'd gone through, clutching his candles, looking for someone to hand them to. The Earl's son had taken him on, educating and encouraging him – and all because of Jude's interest in books. A 'protégé', Richard had called him.

The role of Master Curiosity at the feasts was Richard's idea. Jude was to help entertain the King when he visited Crowbury Hall. Whenever Jude performed, he became more than the stinking son of a candle-maker. For a few moments, people thought well of him. He wanted more of that feeling of respect. It was the stuff of his dreams.

During their rehearsals, Richard always reassured Jude when his tongue tripped over his words. He would even pass on the compliments guests had made at previous events. This astonished and delighted Jude. Richard treated him so well – almost as a younger brother, or a son. And each time he introduced him as Master Curiosity, Jude held his chin a little higher.

Yet this time, ever since he had awoken to find the top page of his notes run and ruined, he felt nothing but a hopeless swirl of confusion. And fear. He did not understand what was happening to him. He felt a shadow of himself. Tears threatened. He felt as though someone had walked over his grave.

The door swung open, and a courtier beckoned energetically.

It was time.

Jude looked around frantically for Richard but the courtier warned that the King would not be kept waiting. Taking a deep breath, he leant his whole weight against the Armillary Sphere and rolled it into the boisterous, feasting crowd, trundling towards the dais at the head of the room with King Henry's table. He did not dare glance up.

The wheels caught on a rug.

He pushed and shoved, but the Sphere would not budge. If he pushed any harder, it would topple over.

"Someone help the goof, for goodness sake!"

Jude quickly scanned the room for Richard. Still no sign. He turned to see hands on the Sphere, more on the wooden base.

"Over 'ere, that's right," Jude murmured.

The servants edged the wheels over the crease in the rug and moved the Sphere into position opposite the King, closer to his imposing presence.

Someone's eyes were boring into him. It was the Earl of Crowbury, his face like thunder. Jude's stomach lurched. It would be his grubby clothes. But Jude could not help it! His Master Curiosity outfit had been immaculate when he'd pulled it on, and he wished he could speak up for himself – the storm was not his fault! But it was impossible. Jude rubbed his sweaty palms on his breeches and wiped his forehead, but this only made things worse by smearing mud onto his face. In his anxiety, he frantically wiped it again. If Richard were here, he would have fetched fresh clothes and helped him clean up before he started – the other servants had been too busy to help. Richard would have made him feel more relaxed, even now. But his friend was nowhere to be seen. The Earl impatiently cast around the room, doubtless thinking the same.

The other guests settled down on long benches, grabbing food from platters on the tables. The King was seated on the usual ornate armchair. Out of the corner of his eye, Jude saw the monarch reach out and hook a passing servant girl by the wrist, pulling her down to his level. He whispered into her ear while coiling a lock of her hair around his fingers, which were covered in jewels like dew-sparkled blackberries. In his fur-trimmed jacket, he looked even more a majestic lion of a man, with finely slashed doublets of green and red velvet, and his shirt embroidered with golden thread. Despite the girl's polite struggles, the King would not let her go, pulling her down closer and touching his lips to her hair. She blushed at the kiss, slipped her hand out of his grip and took a step backwards. The King was amused and the others followed his lead, smiling at the girl's embarrassment.

Jude was relieved at the slight delay. Maybe it was a chance for Richard to appear? But he did not. There was no sign of Richard's beautiful sister, Mary, either. Surely she should be seated nearby?

Finally, the King turned towards Jude, raising an eyebrow. Laughter and conversation died away at the prospect of the night's final entertainment.

Jude bowed low. "Your M-M-Majesty . . ." he stuttered. He flushed and winced at the sound of his own voice.

"Don't worry boy, I shan't eat you. My stomach is full enough from the feast!"

The King chuckled at his own joke and everyone joined in, the ripple of laughter echoing around the chamber. The Earl looked around for his son one last time, irritated. This could wait no longer. An introduction needed to be made. He cleared his throat and stood up to face the King.

"Most Gracious Sovereign. Once again, Crowbury Hall is proud to present Master Curiosity," the Earl said, cautiously. "Your Majesty may recall the curiosities he presented on the last occasion: two items that were small enough to fit in one's tunic pocket. The first, an intricate clock that chimed upon the hour. The other, an ingenious little globe that opened to reveal the heavens." The Earl had no problem recalling these curiosities from his own cabinet.

"Yes, I remember," the King said. He turned to Jude. "Now, young Master Curiosity, what intrigue do you hold for me tonight? I see you have an arrangement of the heavens with you."

Jude froze. His heart hammered in his chest. Words still would not come.

6

Silas and Secrets

The wood was dark as hell. Silas listened out for Ruth's footsteps running through the trees towards the hollow – their secret meeting place. A knot in his stomach pulled tighter. Had she noticed his exchange with Betsy on the road? If so, it would make this a lot harder. He should have been more guarded.

He dreaded her arriving and pictured her face, shining with trust. He exhaled, short and sharp.

Muffled footsteps. Here she came.

A tiny light shone out from Crowbury Hall – no doubt another servant carrying candles passing by a window – casting her figure into deeper shadow as she rushed towards him. There was no time to think. He held out his arms and she ran into them, but he did not hold her tight as he usually would. She lifted her sweet mouth towards him and he half-kissed her – half on the lips and half on her cheek. Her long, lovely, unruly dark hair tumbled over his chest as she pressed herself against him.

"I'd . . . I should be polishing spoons," he said, stupidly.

"And instead you're running away with the family silver." She grinned, looking up at him.

Silas tensed. In a few minutes she would know his intentions – and how ironic her wit would seem then. He couldn't speak. He turned away and sat down on a fallen tree, vigorously wiping

21

away the snow with his hand. Ruth joined him, gathering up her skirts so she could sit close to him.

He drew breath.

Ruth reached into her pocket, pulled something out and gave it to him. It was a book. "Here, another for you."

Was her voice a little tight? Silas was not sure.

He touched the leather cover and traced the embossed words with his fingertip. Her kindness shamed him and he felt angry that this would make everything harder.

But he was stuck, and this was the only way out he could see.

"'Tis Frobisher's travels," Ruth explained. "No tales of monsters and knights and maidens." She leant against his shoulder in the way that would usually draw him close, but he did not move.

"Frobisher – the gentleman who came last year?" He remembered the famous traveller, one of many great men whom the Earl welcomed to the Hall. Silas noted every detail of these adventurers whose lives were infinitely larger than his own.

Ruth nodded.

"I'm grateful. I'll return it before long."

"So you can devour another in even less time," she teased, kissing his shoulder.

"The words show me other worlds . . ." He suddenly saw this was the perfect opening for him. "Ruth, I must say it. I'm minded to leave Crowbury."

Her body started in fright. "No!"

Silas looked down at his hands and he felt her dark eyes upon him. He could not bear to look at her.

"But why?"

Silas shrugged. He spoke half the truth. "Here I'm just an estate hand. I'm . . ."

"No you are not!"

Her fiery nature – he loved that about her. But he could not falter.

"But I am," he pressed on. "In London I'd make something of myself, learn a trade, find an apprenticeship." He pointed at the book she had given him. "A bookbinder, Ruth! I could print words and let more folk see beyond their own small lives. I've thought often about this. The feeling grows with every book you lend me."

Ruth shook her head and almost laughed. "You mean I've helped to drive you away?"

Silas could say nothing. In a sense, it was true.

"But you've always been in my life!" The words burst out of her.

Silas drifted away . . . back to summer afternoons chasing Ruth through meadows of swaying grasses, bewitched by her swinging dark curls . . . her delight as they went scrumping apples in orchards . . . that dove they caught and kept in the hayloft till, one day, the bird found a gap in the thatch and together they had watched it fly free.

There had been nothing strange about their friendship then. Nothing complicated. But so much had changed. Too much. Back then, both she and the Earl were grieving the loss of a mother and a wife. Ruth was the beloved daughter of the house who was allowed to roam free with all the servants' children. But the Earl had since remarried, and the Countess and her children had arrived at Crowbury Hall with her Steward in tow. Now the Steward ruled the roost – Ruth's father had, in effect, let him do it. The Earl had turned a blind eye, taking himself away on business to the far corners of the globe. Whenever he returned, it was never for long.

The place was not what it had been.

Silas knew the Steward disliked him; the man would never let him get on. No chance of advancement or more responsibility.

And in the past month, Silas sensed the Steward's suspicion of him and Ruth . . .

But that was not the half of it, though he would not admit as much to Ruth.

Silas felt a cheat for pinning the blame for his decision on the Countess and the Steward, but he would do it nevertheless. It would hurt Ruth less than knowing the real quandary he faced with Betsy.

Passing Betsy in the lane earlier, he'd taken a risk – to mislead the Steward about him and Ruth. In reality, the Steward was the greater problem for his whole family. Silas just hoped that Ruth would not question him.

He became aware that she was looking pointedly at the ground, not watching him, trying to remain dignified. Seeing her pride, he felt suddenly drawn to her. Betsy was never like this.

Moments passed. He watched her in the darkness.

At last Ruth closed her eyes briefly and sat up straighter. She wiped away a tear with her finger.

"Ruth," he said, finding the courage. "What we have . . . it can go no further."

"Silas!" Ruth cried, her voice sharp with alarm.

In the darkness, she could barely see his expression. It made things a little easier for him, but not much.

"But you love me! You have told me so. Countless times!"

Silas could not say he did or he didn't. He no longer knew. He felt ashamed but out of duty to her he wouldn't cut this short, not quite yet. He'd finish the words he had planned.

"Ruth, you must know the Countess won't have this – us."

He spoke the words firmly but gently. After a moment, he took her hands in his own. They were trembling.

"My stepmother may have power but she cannot stop our hearts!" There was a tremble in her voice, too.

He said nothing but rubbed her hands.

"Nothing can," she insisted.

Silas winced. The treachery was almost unbearable.

She was crying more, now, which tugged at his heart and confused him further. He wiped away her tear. Her skin was so soft.

"Come, now," he said gently.

At this little gesture she looked up, hopeful. He had to dash it again.

"The Steward knows," he said. "I am sure of it. He will tell the Countess – if he hasn't already."

She nodded. "He's at my heels every place I go! But he has no power over me. And our closeness hurts no-one."

To Silas, her comment was easy to refute but hard to say. "Your bloodline and mine . . . the Countess will think mine will sully yours . . . she will be thinking of her own daughters and their prospects."

She paused. "Oh. I had not thought . . . so far ahead." Her voice sounded shy. Silas knew that her womanhood had not yet come, unlike Betsy, who had made that perfectly clear. "But my stepsisters are so young! And surely these decisions are between me and my father . . ."

"Your stepbrother Charles is almost ready to be wed," Silas reminded her.

"Doubtless it was he who told the Steward to spy on us," Ruth spoke as if the words tasted sour in her mouth.

"Perhaps . . . Ruth, you and I will not fit with the Countess's plans."

Ruth shook her head.

"Come on, Ruth, you must know this already – we wouldn't be a secret if it were not so."

She paused and breathed deeply. "But if I spoke to father, Silas . . . he would consent to us being together."

"I doubt it. Would he go against his own wife?"

"Would he deny his own daughter? Mother was free to be with *him*! Father was a mere merchant but Grandfather Richard saw how much they loved one another, despite their inequalities. How could he deny *me* the same freedom?"

A *mere* merchant! The words rang in Silas's ears. That position was infinitely more privileged than his own. She had unwittingly played into his hands.

"A merchant, not a servant boy like me. It's hardly the same," Silas stood up. "I must go, Ruth."

"Silas, what's happened to you? All those things we've spoken of so many times, how on the inside servants are the same as nobility, the same sense and feeling, the same flesh and blood!"

"But you read Latin, French . . . you know astronomy, cosmology . . ."

"Stop it! You've made your point. You know they mean nothing to me, Silas."

"You'd tire of me."

"No, I would not! What am I to do with all that learning? Stitch myself a better life? You used to say that we were the same, you and I."

It was true – he had believed that. "It was a childish thing to say."

"Oh Silas, will you not have it, that I love you?"

He felt a sudden fierce fondness for her. Had he made the wrong decision? He looked up into the branches of the tree above, to the black clouds beyond.

She reached out and touched his jacket. He put his hand on hers, and pulled her up towards him, close. At the smell of her, something in him crumpled. He rested his hands on her waist, felt the small curve towards her hips – the way she was changing into a young woman.

"Five years . . . it'd be five years from now, if I waited till after my apprenticeship," he mumbled. "Perhaps then I'd be more worthy."

"You are worthy as you are," she countered, lifting her chin.

He felt overcome by her belief in him and kissed her, full and soft, and leant his forehead against hers.

Ruth pressed her face into his neck and breathed in deeply, as if drinking him in, and he succumbed further and buried his face in her hair.

"So all is well?"

He gave no answer but caressed her waist through her cape.

He was back with Betsy. That kiss.

Suddenly he pictured his shining hunting knife in his right hand, as if the flat of it was pressed against Ruth's back.

The image – his power to hurt her – revolted him. He stepped away.

"I must leave. Those spoons await my attention," he said. He was trying to be playful.

"Oh but a few moments more!" She drew close again.

"I'll be missed, Ruth."

"It's so dark, the moon's gone," she said, ignoring his comment, refusing to let him go. "Just whispers of sounds." Her breath was hot on his neck.

He stood there, hands dropped to his sides. His feet were deep in the snow which cast an unearthly light. Against it, she was a pool of black. Scores of tree trunks caged them in. The wind was building in the great branches high above.

A twig snapped nearby.

Another snapped, a little closer.

A deep grunt.

"Run!" Silas was dashing away from her and she followed, slipping on icy stones, leaping over the frozen stream, running up towards the haw-haw. Panting, he scrambled up the steep slope onto the safety of the lawn and pulled her up behind him. They turned to peer in the direction from which they had run. Thundering hooves came closer and they saw a pair of small eyes, reflecting light from the windows. It was a wild boar. Unwilling to break cover from the wood, it hesitated for a moment, then turned and ran back through the trees.

"We frightened it," said Silas.

He looked at her, the lights from the Hall gently illuminating the side of her face. Snowflakes drifted down and fell between them. Ruth's focus changed from his face to one falling flake. She watched it float down, and shivered.

"You're cold," he whispered.

She shook her head. "No, no, not really."

"Spoons."

"Spoons . . ." Ruth smiled, and let him go.

7

A Fateful Misjudgement

King Henry strode over to the Armillary Sphere. Hands on hips, he surveyed the contraption. His head cocked to one side as he looked closer. All around were silent, waiting for the King's reaction.

Jude bowed a little and moved out of his way, his head low, scanning the legs of the guests in the hope of seeing Richard's.

He could not have felt more unprepared for this moment.

On the edge of his sight, he could see the King peering through the brass circles at the small globes representing the Sun and the Moon. At the centre of it all was Earth, finely painted in greens and blues.

"Fine craftsmanship," the King remarked. As he passed by Jude, he grimaced and waved his hand in front of his nose. He had caught a whiff of tallow.

At this, a few guests tittered.

Jude's guts clenched. Already things were different to last time.

The King spotted the wooden handle. His curiosity aroused, he reached down and turned it. The wheels of the Armillary Sphere began to rotate, causing the globes to move in synchronicity. Murmuring conversation stopped. All eyes were on this incredible moving work of art. No-one had seen such a machine before. It was the universe sprung to life. Circles rotated within turning circles as planets and stars slowly spun around the Earth.

"And everything, naturally, revolves around us," the King said, with a degree of satisfaction in his voice.

Jude cleared his throat.

"Well, p'raps not," he said under his breath, flushing furiously. "Your-your most excellent Royal Majesty." He hastily added the appropriate form of address.

"Perhaps *not*?" The King's eyes flicked over to Jude.

Jude took a deep breath. He was swamped by dread that he was wading into disaster. Yet he couldn't stop himself any more than he could stop a river overflowing.

"I'm waiting."

Jude forced himself to speak the first words that came into his mind. "Your Majesty, um, there are questioning thoughts abroad."

The banqueting chamber was silent.

"Thoughts? Not just one but *two* thoughts. And what might these *thoughts* be?"

The King returned to his table and sat down heavily in his chair with a thump. He stared at Jude impassively, clearly expecting a dull response from this scrawny, mud-splattered boy.

Jude had to engage with him. There was no way out.

"Tis . . . um . . ." He reached inside his pocket for his sodden notes, and held them out. A drip of water fell to the floor. "See, Your Majesty, after making my candles . . . I . . . excuse me . . . my head tumbles like a hedgehog."

Jude heard a barely repressed titter of laughter from the audience.

"Get to your point." The King's voice was brisk.

Jude breathed deeply, trying to control his sense of panic. He placed his notes on the Armillary Sphere's stand, grabbed the handle and turned it around vigorously, rotating star after planet after star, much too fast. Richard's father sat up in alarm.

"See – the Earth does not stray from its spot, but . . ."

"Yes – and your point *is*?" Everybody sensed that the King's patience was wearing thin.

More words rushed back – but were they the right or the wrong words? Jude did not know, and blurted them out.

"Begging your pardon Majesty, but p'raps it ain't true, 'cos these orbs of heavenly light are beautiful but . . ." Jude shook his head.

The King leant forwards in his chair. *"But?"*

"But p'raps our planet isn't as still as a dead pig. P'raps it turns round and round like an apple rolling downhill – 'tis how night follows day."

Jude scratched his head. *What* was the name of that radical man? He thought of Richard's little painted globe, dangling on its golden chain. That natural philosopher from Poland . . . his name was on the tip of Jude's tongue. He almost had it.

"Co . . . coperni . . . Oh! Never mind! P'raps *we're* not at the centre of the heavens, but the *Sun* is?"

Jude looked down at his feet.

The silence was deafening.

And when Jude picked up the courage to look at the King's face, the monarch did not appear intrigued or impressed. He was angry. Jude began to tremble, realising that these were the wrong words. Yet still more cascaded out of his mouth. He had to explain himself. He had to please the King.

"'Tis as if the Sun is on the royal throne and all the other lesser planets and stars circle around him—"

"Enough!" The King held up his hand and glared. "How extraordinary. You're actually suggesting that the Sun is at the centre of the heavens – not the Earth! And that our planet is turning?"

Jude nodded. "Not me. 'Tis Coperni . . . oh, I cannot remember his name. But don't you see? It's like we used to think the world was flat and if we sailed too far we'd drop off, but then Master Magellan—"

"You dare argue with me? King, Commander of Church and State! You dare argue with Aristotle and the Holy Book?" The King seemed to grow in stature, his face set with fury.

"I'm not argui—"

"Silence! If the Earth were *turning* we'd all fall over! No! The Earth is still: that is sense of the common kind, as you put it. We are at the centre of the heavens. Plainly, it is the most important planet because we are on it. God placed it here in prime position. The Moon and the Sun and the stars all know their place. Unlike some others!"

Jude shook his head. He looked around. Sneering, mocking faces surrounded him. Where *was* Richard? He always knew the right thing to say. His head swimming, he searched the faces of the crowd. He looked back at the King.

"Your Majesty is a most learned man . . ."

"I said SILENCE! What you, you of so little learning, are saying is blasphemy. You arrogantly exalt your thoughts above the authorities!" The King's eyes widened with every word he spoke, and spittle formed at the edges of his mouth.

Jude trembled and shook his head.

"You dare to challenge me?" the King thundered, standing up. "When you challenge my God-given authority, you challenge the very authority of God Himself. There is heresy in what you say. Take his notes!"

Jude was breathless, terrified. Heresy was punishable by death: he could be burnt at the stake! He held his notes close to his chest but a servant yanked them out of his hands and passed them to the King, who held them between his thumb and forefinger as though they might contaminate the royal hand.

"Yet you are nothing. These are a mess." The King shook his head. Then, as if turning on a penny, his temper deserted him. He glanced at the Earl of Crowbury. "And this is meant to be a feast."

King Henry tossed Jude's damp papers into the fireplace behind him, where they hit the flames with a sizzle of steam. He turned to a servant nearby, demanding that his tankard be refilled. The murmuring of conversation in the chamber resumed as the crisis seemed to have passed, though Jude could hear snake tongues whispering.

The Earl of Crowbury, his face scarlet, strode over to where Jude stood.

"Get out!" the Earl spat. "And whatever my son tells you in the future, never darken Crowbury Hall again. You're lower than a commoner, destined to crawl upon the Earth and suck the mud!" He turned on his heel and returned to the table.

For a moment, Jude couldn't move, paralysed by the Earl's words.

His notes in the fireplace were engulfed by bright flames. Orange tongues raced, nullifying each word and mark he had made, reducing his work to black flakes that swirled and twisted furiously before disappearing up the chimney.

He was horrified. The brightness with which he had penned those words . . . the hope of Richard's friendship lifting him out of the dregs, the hope of an end to the bullying, his father's violence . . .

As the fire died down, the last flickering light of hope inside Jude was snuffed out too, his dreams with them.

He blinked, his eyes full of tears, and looked up to see Richard. Richard!

8

The Secrets of Books

Ruth tingled as she sprinted across the snowy lawn. So Silas had spoken of marriage! It had come about strangely, but nevertheless, he had said it in as many words. If only she could shake off that dream – even just a moment ago black snow had flitted across her vision. It haunted her. The lingering uneasiness was spoiling the happiness she should surely be feeling.

She glanced at the footprints her boots were leaving behind in the snow. The coming storm would cover them. She need not worry.

A candle ghosted past a window. Servants hurried back and forth in the banqueting chamber, still clearing up. She dipped down low to avoid being seen, and bristled at the thought of the Countess and Steward, orchestrating everything. She had no idea that the pair of them affected Silas so badly. She hated them now, for the way they made him feel. They had almost broken his love.

Ruth slowed down where the lawn fell away steeply behind the Hall. Her foot slipped. She grabbed a holly bush, flinching at its thorns. Finally, she reached the doorway hidden behind the bush, edged it open, squeezed through, pulled it tight shut and climbed the steps. Up above, a chink of light came from her bedchamber. There was the faint sound of someone rapping their knuckles on a door, growing louder the closer she came. It was a blessing she had remembered to turn the key and lock it. Hurrying towards the secret panel that led into her room, she stumbled over the banned books her father had hidden long ago – and as she did so, an idea occurred to her.

"Miss Ruth!" Nurse's voice penetrated through the thick wood of her door. She was not usually so shrill.

Ruth edged the wooden panel along, squeezed through the gap and replaced it firmly behind her. She pulled the chair over, hiding the entrance to the secret stairway. Brushing away the cobwebs and snow, she threw down her cape, pulled off her boots and put them beside the fireplace, tousled her hair to make it look as though she had been taking a nap.

"Just a moment!"

The knocking continued relentlessly. She turned the key. Nurse burst in.

"Countess wants you!" Nurse's cheeks were flushed and the stray brown curls escaping her cap shook as she spoke.

"I doubt that very much," Ruth smirked. With Nurse, she never had to guard her sarcasm. She pulled out the top bow of the ribbon on her gown.

"She insists on seeing you at six o'clock sharp," said Nurse, loosening the gown. "Says she's exhausted with all the sortings-out after the feast and wants to be early to eat, even earlier to bed, if that were possible!"

"So she is not content." Ruth chose a simple evening dress from her hanging cupboard and dropped it over her head.

"When is she ever, Miss Ruth?" Nurse tut-tutted as she helped. "This is tight, young lady – ribbons are getting short – you need new dresses, but it will do for her ladyship. Where've you been anyway? Steward said he was here a while ago."

Ruth rolled her eyes. It was best to say nothing.

Nurse neatened Ruth's hair and touched her forehead with the back of her hand, as she always did, out of habit. "But you're hot – heavens, child, your head is burning! I must fetch some herbs!"

"I am perfectly well, thank you, Nurse." Ruth turned her head away and glanced at her boots. "It was just the skating today, that's all."

"Hmmph." Nurse finished tying the ribbon into a bow and smiled. "There you go again, telling me off for my prating and mithering!" She fiddled with bits of her charge's dress, pulled at a loose thread and snapped it off. "Don't be late for her! You know how she gets."

"I wonder what she wants now? Am I to order more silks for her tapestry, even though that's the Housekeeper's job . . ." Ruth giggled at Nurse's appalled expression and swung her body around her bedpost, playing Maypole. "Fetch some meadow-sweet, for it is Queen Elizabeth's new favourite . . ." Ruth swung again.

"Miss Ruth, watch that tongue of yours! Now hurry, please . . ." Nurse kissed her on the cheek and left the room.

Ruth glanced at the wooden panel hiding her secrets. Stumbling over those books had made her think of *The Distinction of Dreams* in the library, which she had read last year. There were so many books there, and this one had slipped her mind. Surely it could help her now, and give her a proper interpretation of black snow. If she could understand it, perhaps the horrible feeling would go away. Her stepmother could wait.

Ruth left her bedchamber and dashed down the stairs towards the library. It was the place she most liked in the whole of Crowbury Hall. It was a cathedral of ideas – thousands of thoughts written on thousands of pages.

As she opened the door, she hesitated. Her stepsisters were sitting around the fireplace. Anna's eyebrows lifted and she brightened to see Ruth then went back to sucking her thumb while playing with the cloth doll Ruth had made for her. Eleanor, the eldest, barely looked up as she pushed a needle in and out of a square of embroidery. Margaret hummed a tune to herself and tapped her foot and twirled her hair, lost in some other world. Her stepbrother was not there. The girls would usually be with their mother at this time of day; the Countess must have a headache.

Eleanor looked up, bored. "Is supper ready?"

"I know not," replied Ruth. "Good eve," she added pointedly. She held out an arm for Anna, who rushed into her skirts.

"Goodest eve to you, Ruthie," said Anna, pulling her thumb out of her mouth.

Ruth knelt down and embraced her.

"Hello dear thing – and hello to you too," said Ruth, addressing both Anna and her doll. Anna giggled, and Ruth fondly tapped the tip of her nose and kissed her cheek, then did the same for her doll.

"Decorum, Anna," Eleanor warned. The little girl immediately returned to Eleanor's side.

Ruth smirked. Eleanor was increasingly a parrot for her mother. "She is only three," Ruth said quietly.

"Still," replied Eleanor, turning back to her embroidery.

Eleanor was a cold fish. She rarely played with her sisters, let alone Little Luce and other children around the place. It had been just the same last night at the feast. Ruth had played with Little Luce, blowing bubbles into her palm to make her giggle and soon the Crowbury children were all queuing for their turn. Inevitably, Anna was kept firmly at the Countess's side.

Ruth began to hunt for *The Distinction of Dreams*. She started at one end of the room above their Cabinet of Curiosities and looked all along the shelves, past the harpsichord, past the old

Armillary Sphere, scanning the titles on all the shelves and piles of books on the floor. She paused briefly. Was this wise – what if the interpretation brought no end to her uneasiness but just made it worse? Her finger hesitated over the spine of a manuscript. Books did have a habit of turning things on their head. But knowing was always better than not knowing. The search continued.

As she worked her way along a row, she remembered how one radical book came to be hidden in the secret panel behind her bed. It was the last time John Dee and Thomas Digges had come to visit her father, bringing navigational equipment for his next voyage. John Dee's library was the biggest in the kingdom so the gift of a book was nothing unusual. But this one was different. She remembered Digges fumbling in his bag and unveiling it, lowering his voice so that no-one with an ear to the door could hear. Father signalled with a nod that Ruth could stay. Digges whispered its title: *The Prognostication Everlasting of Right Good Effect*.

Ruth was riveted by what Digges said next.

He had been gripped by Copernicus's banned theory from 1543 about the location of the Earth in the universe, and had set about mathematically proving or disproving it. His findings vindicated Copernicus, running against the belief of the whole of Christendom. The scientific proof was all there on these pages, Digges said, turning the leaves of the book. In the silence, the pages flicked so loudly. She remembered her father's eyes, so wide, staring at his guest. This was heresy. Enough for a burning!

Her father looked at John Dee, who nodded in support of his friend, and smiled. Ruth lowered her eyes, scanning the lines of her book without taking them in, thrilled by their undaunted curiosity and courage.

As soon as the visitors left, she and her father sat and read the *Prognostication* from cover to cover. Father had stressed that people in authority would feel threatened by the ideas proposed – and this was why Copernicus had been banned during the reign of King Henry the Eighth. He strongly warned Ruth not to show Digges's book to a soul – not even to her tutor. They hid it behind the secret panel, where Copernicus's theory was already hidden, an old tatty amateur copy. Long ago, Grandfather Richard had burnt the original to be safe.

At last, she found *The Distinction of Dreams* and settled in a chair to read it. She ran her finger down the index. Black snow was not listed. She leafed through the book, trying to find anything that could help her understand. There was nothing. And at that very moment, the dream returned, darker than ever.

The black sky empties itself. Shadows falling without end.

Unease settled thickly upon her.

She closed the book and leant her head against the wings of the chair, her eyelids suddenly heavy.

A moment later, the door swung open and Charles marched into the room. The top of the door caught the feather plume of his new hat, pushing it backwards. He corrected its tilt. Ruth suppressed a smile, glad of a distraction from her uncomfortable feelings.

"The Countess is waiting," he announced, standing before her in his most commanding manner. His new jacket drew attention to itself. Military-style, over a ruff, and all a tad large. It emphasised his thin frame in an unfortunate way, though he showed no sign of realising it.

"Yes, of course," Ruth replied. She stood up.

Charles led the way to the Withdrawing Room. Ruth resented

having to follow at his heels, the more so because she knew how much her stepbrother enjoyed it.

Her stepmother sat beside the blazing fireplace at the far end, casting a long shadow that danced over the new, red silk-covered wall like a moving fresco: a scene from Dante's hellish Inferno.

9

The Announcement

"Come, child." The Countess was a dark silhouette against the fire. Her eyes reflected the flames and glittered.

"You wanted to see me?" Ruth stepped closer.

The Countess wore a new blue gown over a matching bodice and skirt, and a new figure-of-eight ruff, made with the finest Italian lace. A pomander dangled from her hand and she sniffed occasionally into a handkerchief. Charles joined his mother and leant against the fireplace while he spoke quietly to her. All the time, her eyes remained on Ruth.

"You have regained your composure since last night?" she finally asked.

"Pardon me?" Ruth stifled a smile. Had the Countess called her here just to reprimand her? She always made it perfectly clear that she didn't approve of Ruth's friendliness with the lower born – perhaps Ruth had crossed another line.

The Countess raised an eyebrow. It had been a hypothetical question. "I have news for you," she said.

For a moment Ruth's heart lifted at the prospect of a letter from her father, but the look on her stepmother's face indicated something entirely different.

The Countess sniffed into her handkerchief.

"It is with regard to your security. I'm sure you know that our Hall and estate shall pass entirely to my dear Charles when your father dies, as is customary."

Ruth swayed. She had always known this could happen but her stepmother had never mentioned it before.

Charles's face twitched. He looked at the fire, although he watched Ruth out of the corner of his eye. She was careful to keep any emotion out of her face.

"So, clearly, you cannot linger here any longer than necessary," the woman continued.

"Have you bad news of father?" Ruth asked quickly, before the full meaning of the Countess's words hit her.

"Nothing of that nature." She shifted in her seat. "Well, then. I feared I would have difficulty finding the appropriate suitor."

Blood rushed to Ruth's face. She could not conceal her alarm. It seemed as though time slowed down as she realised what the Countess was about to say. A husband! Her stepmother was capable of many things, but never had Ruth imagined this.

"Come," the Countess beckoned, smiling icily. She offered Ruth a small oval portrait in an ornate gold frame. "I have been searching for some time on your behalf. Here. Come." She pressed the miniature portrait a little too hard into Ruth's hand.

As Ruth saw it, she was almost sick. The man was older than her father! In her shock, Ruth let the portrait slip through her fingers. It clattered to the floor. The Countess clicked her tongue.

"But – but I am still a girl!"

Charles knelt and picked up the painting, replacing it in his mother's lap.

"Look at how your figure is changing. Your sheets are watched. It is surely only a month or so before your womanhood comes."

Her bed sheets! They were checking for the first signs of blood! She flushed and took a step back.

Charles coughed daintily.

"And then," the Countess continued, "you shall be ripe enough for a husband's plucking. This is a good likeness. His name is

Lord Boswell and he is willing to take you as a wife. He has a title, a good estate in Cheshire. You must stop your ridiculous reading straightaway so your fertility can recover."

The words hung in the air between herself and the Countess. Moments passed. Ruth realised her legs were shaking.

The corner of the Countess's mouth turned up in a sadistic curl.

"At fifteen you will satisfy his desires. He requires a male heir."

The words came at Ruth, sharp as daggers. Her eyes stung and she fiercely tried to keep back her tears.

"I beg you . . ."

"You beg my leave, to reflect upon your good fortune to have been chosen by such a noble man. No?"

Ruth shook her head, not in answer but in terror. Plucked against her will, and by such a man as this.

"My father agrees?" Her mouth felt so dry she could barely speak.

Her stepmother stared at the flames. "My husband left all estate decisions to me in his absence."

"*Estate?* I am not a piece of property!"

"Oh my dear, on the contrary," the Countess replied. "It turns out that you *are* of some value – 'property' is entirely appropriate."

"That cannot be right! You cannot do this! Not without father's say-so."

"That is the law, is it not, Charles?" The Countess stood up, looking to her son. He did not respond and would not meet his mother's eye. "The judge said so," she continued, turning to face Ruth. "The bishop will grant a marriage licence as my husband is overseas . . . after all, there's no date for his return."

Charles knelt down, grabbed a pair of tongs and turned a log, which disintegrated into ash, red embers spilling everywhere. He kicked them back into the fireplace.

"Besides," the Countess continued, sitting down. "If your education has been of any worth at all, you will come to see that this is quite a satisfying solution."

"You speak as though there is a problem that needs a solution," snapped Ruth, "but there is none, save for the one in your imagination."

"The *problem* is a person, and my solution is neat. Lord Boswell seems confident that he will bring about some semblance of correct behaviour." She paused, sniffed into her handkerchief, and added casually: "This comet and others you have spoken of repeatedly to your tutor, the, what was it?"

"*Stupendum Dei Miraculum*," replied Ruth, frowning. So her tutor had been reporting on their conversations. Father had been right to be cautious about him. What else did the Countess know?

"Yes, well. You were born in the year of this comet – I have consulted an astrologer – it signified anarchy, so perhaps it is not such a surprise that you are a wild child." The Countess almost beamed in self-congratulation at using Ruth's own interests against her.

"But father brought me up in a natural way and gave me certain liberties, that is all."

"So you say, but it is more than that. There is something of the maverick in you, and that is not becoming in a young woman. You are an aberration of nobility." The Countess paused, watching Ruth digest her words. "The true *miraculum* is that Boswell knows of your spirited nature but is willing to take you on. I know he likes wild creatures. Especially horses. He likes to tame them. Break them." The Countess made no attempt to conceal a triumphant smile.

Ruth's head swarmed with angry words. She felt weak and strong at the same time. She felt like collapsing. Running away. Slapping the woman hard.

"Don't look so troubled, dear. Your chart also shows you will redeem yourself with a purposeful destiny."

In that moment, Ruth knew that her fate with Boswell was sealed.

Silas was lost to her, as was her home. Her life was broken.

"How dare you!" She couldn't muster any further words.

Her stepmother looked amused.

"Perhaps you would like to take a seat?" said Charles feebly, indicating the chair close by.

"NO!" Ruth grabbed the chair and threw it clattering across the floorboards, and as it crashed into the wall she turned to face her stepmother, breathing heavily. The Countess cried out. Charles stepped in front of his mother.

The two young people faced one another.

Ruth steadied her breathing and stared into Charles's narrowed eyes, teeming with hatred. Then, as if he drew a mask over, his face became expressionless again. He was already so Machiavellian. Just like his mother.

The Countess smoothed the silk of her dress and regained her composure. "Well, well."

Her fists clenched, Ruth strode back and forth. "So father knows nothing of your plan?"

"I see no reason why he would object. Lord Boswell is well liked at Court. My husband knows I have always planned to rectify the loss suffered after your great-aunt threw away her chance with King Henry. Your marriage would change everything. The Queen would be pleased."

Grandfather Richard's sister Mary had died young, in childbirth. Ruth knew she had been a great beauty and was much admired for her kindness, like her brother. It was shocking that the Countess had mentioned the incident with King Henry. Her grandfather had written about it, but it had been nothing more than a passing moment one afternoon – and it had been unwelcome.

"You assume an intimacy with my family's past as though you yourself were born a Henryson, but you were not," Ruth said, barely concealing her anger.

At this, her stepmother got up, approached Ruth, and slapped her across the face.

"Insolent child!"

Ruth resisted the urge to put her hand to her cheek. Anger flared.

The woman sat down again and settled her gaze on Ruth.

"As your father's wife, I *am* a Henryson. It has grieved me that Queen Elizabeth has never accepted my invitation to stay. Your marriage into the Boswells will correct matters and preserve the integrity of this line. You should be grateful, child. Besides, my husband always does as I ask."

So her life was being sacrificed for her stepmother's ambition.

"You know very well that father cares little for Court, though he is naturally devoted to the Queen," Ruth lifted her chin. "*He* does not seek favour."

"Which is why the Queen has never come to visit. My husband acts the gentleman, not the Earl, and I intend to rectify that through Boswell. The matter is decided. It would be better for everyone if you left Crowbury Hall . . . and the sooner the better." The Countess's voice hardened. "For are there not certain clandestine associations that must end?"

Silas!

Ruth held her breath.

The Countess and Charles exchanged glances.

So the Steward had shared his suspicions! How the Countess relished her power over her stepdaughter. Ruth blinked fast to stop a tear from falling – she would not give the woman the satisfaction of seeing her cry.

"So you must leave. And calm yourself, child. You will become no use to anyone if you become frantic."

Ruth wanted to shout out that Crowbury was *her* home. But she said not a word more. She turned on her heel and ran towards the door, glimpsing the bulk of a man standing in the shadows, his beady eyes catching the firelight. The Steward. She should have known. He would have heard the whole conversation, and doubtless had prior knowledge of the Countess's plans.

Ruth ran down the long gallery, past the recently commissioned portraits and busts which were all part of her stepmother's plans to rearrange the world in her favour. Father's merchant wealth, coupled with his title, played into her hands to perfection. Her scheming would change the family beyond recognition. As if it were her own court, she would have swarms of attendants and be served by the sons of gentlemen. Before long she would have a bell rung in her honour as she moved through Crowbury, and all lower-born men would have to remove their hats as she passed. And Ruth would be nowhere to be seen.

IO

A Soul Stolen

In the doorway to the banqueting chamber, staring straight at Jude, was Richard. He looked aghast.

"What . . .?"

He saw Richard mouth the word, soundless above the guests' conversation.

Then he felt the King's eyes upon him and, like a shamed dog, he met the King's stare.

"Fool."

At this final condemnation, Jude fled.

He ran along the passageway towards the staircase, dashing down the steps. Above his quick sharp breaths and scampering feet, he heard shouts. There were footsteps behind him. Terrified, he hurtled towards the doorway, his shoulder colliding with another servant on the way, sending a platter of food to the ground. He slammed into the exit to the garden, frantically turned the lock, yanked open the heavy door and ran out into the night.

Seeing the maze of bushes, he ducked into the greenery, crawling in deeper until he felt hidden. Voices shouted as they searched for him. His body sank into cold mud. It coated his face and clothes and seeped into his shoes. Half-choking on tears and a mouthful of soil, he tried to calm his breathing. Eventually, the voices retreated back inside the house. They would come after him at first light, he was sure.

Where could he go? He had been utterly humiliated. All dignity and hope had disappeared from his future in just one night. He could not face any more cruelty. He just couldn't bear it. He was never good enough, never clever enough, never fast enough, never clean enough. Lying there, filthy and soaking, he wanted to rage against every mocking word ever said against him, every cruel insult spoken by his father, by the whole town. Inside, he screamed and screamed. With every thump of his heart, despair burned into him. It devoured any remaining thought of goodness and hope until nothing was left except black bitterness and a grief so deep he felt he was bursting with pain.

Jude wiped his eyes.

He had to get away from here.

He dragged himself over the garden wall into the depths of the wood. Avoiding the main track down which the guests from the feast would make their way home, he stumbled through the trees. Branches tore at his face and pulled at his clothes but he felt nothing. He ran past the church and through the streets and whenever he saw people, took refuge in doorways. He glanced down his own lane. The candle-maker's windows were dark. His father would be in the tavern. Finally, he reached the edge of town. He ran over the crossroads, above which the gibbet hung from a tree. Swinging there was the poacher hung months ago, his remains caught by a gust of wind.

Finally, Jude reached the ruins of the monastery.

Moonlit trees cast shadows that stretched like ragged fingers towards him.

Blinded by grief, Jude did not see the dark shadowy dream thieves that had been following him all along, drawn to his intense despair.

Now the dream thieves swarmed around him, blocking out the moonlight and smothering his body, cloaking him in a creeping darkness that penetrated deep into his soul.

Shaking, the boy sank down onto his haunches, cradling himself against the cold and the hurt, quietly moaning, wrapping his arms tight around his knees, his hands sometimes covering his ears, then his chest, rocking backwards and forwards, until he slowed down, hardly moving.

His body was becoming as still as stone.

The dream thieves screeched like harpies, lit up by the energy of his despair. The thief who had stolen Jude's dream the previous night swooped in and entombed his body in shadows, whispering into his ear.

Words came slowly out of Jude's mouth in a voice that no-one would recognise as his. He muttered them over and over again, cursing himself.

"Better a stone heart than a heart that hurts . . .

Better stone ears than ears that hear . . .

Better a stone soul than a soul that hopes . . .

Stone heart . . . stone ears . . . stone soul . . ."

Shadows on the Stairs

She stretches out her hand to catch a snowflake and there it is, a perfect, tiny black crystal. It melts and swirls on her fingertip like weak black paint. Endless shadows fall from the black sky. She sticks out her tongue to catch another flake. For a moment it rests, a complete crystal, then collapses. It tastes bitter. Her upturned face catches more thick black snowflakes that gather in the hollow of her eyes before she wipes them away. Darkness covers the landscape. She strains to see through the swarm of shadows. Her curiosity shifts to fear. There's no sound, save her quickening breath. Then, a cry of distress. She sees the freezing boy, black snow thick around him, his fingers reaching out for her.

Ruth awoke with a gasp, shivering in the darkness.

She had drifted off to sleep on her bed, fully clothed. Still, even after her stepmother's brutal announcement, that dream had come to her, more powerful than ever.

A storm lashed at her windows.

Her eyes were swollen from tears and her skull throbbed. She pulled the covers over herself, and curled up into a ball. She felt for the little pocket globe and closed her fingers around it.

A soft knocking came at her door, just audible above the wind. A voice whispered her name.

"Miss Ruth!" It was Nurse. She knocked gently again.

Ruth rolled onto her back, pressing her fingers into her forehead where it hurt.

"Please Miss Ruth, you must eat! 'Tis not like you to miss supper."

Clearly the Countess had not yet disclosed her plans to the household – this evil perversion, like the snow in her dream.

In earlier days, Ruth would jump onto Nurse's lap, into her arms and spill out her story. But she was a child no more. Those days had gone.

How could she have been so naïve about the Countess? Silas had been right to worry.

She felt utterly alone.

Ruth looked at the ornate carvings on her four bedposts as though for the first time. They were just discernible in the dark: an ancient ship with billowing sails, great waves, and, on an island, trees with great spikey leaves, and unusual birds. Above the scene, a carved rainbow stretched across the headboard with her parents' initials and profiles in the middle. Mother had designed this bed and her "Paradise Room" using grandfather's descriptions of the New World and his favourite book, *Utopia*. Ever since she was little Ruth had slept here, a nest that held her each night, where mother and father would kiss her goodnight and always tell her to hold fast to her hopes and dreams.

"Miss Ruth . . . Miss Ruth!" Nurse knocked a little louder.

Knowing Nurse would not leave her alone, Ruth relented. "Come," she said.

Nurse opened the door slowly, carrying a candle in one hand, a heel of bread and a tankard in the other. The candlelight fell over Ruth's face. Nurse's eyes widened.

"Oh heavens!"

Nurse set down her things, sat heavily on the edge of the bed and clasped Ruth's hand, waiting for her to speak.

"It's the Countess. She plans a betrothal for me." Hearing herself say the words aloud brought home the full force of their meaning.

Nurse's hand flew to her mouth, her face crumpling. "Oh, Miss! So soon!"

Ruth nodded. "And to Lord Boswell, a detestable old man."

"No!"

Ruth nodded again. "I know him not but I was shown his likeness. He sounds a tyrant – she says he will 'break me like a horse'."

"No! Dearest thing! No!" Nurse moved closer and hugged Ruth tight.

"She plans to send me away." Ruth swept a tear away from her cheek with the back of her hand.

Nurse's familiar curls brushed against her as she shook her head.

"This is too much, too much. I . . . oh . . . You're chilled to the bone, dear child." Nurse retreated to the fire and poked the embers, sniffing loudly.

Nothing was safe, Ruth thought. Nothing sacred from her past. Yes, when the time came and her father died, Charles would inherit every stick and stone, every tree and brick and book of the Crowbury estate. Everything she knew and loved would become his – his property, to do with as he wished. This bed, her tiny globe, even her clothes. But Charles and the Countess were not waiting for events to take a natural course: they were forcing it. More than that, they wanted to destroy her spirit by marrying her to this hideous man. They must hate her so!

"Father does not know, but she believes he would approve!"

"Surely not!" cried Nurse from the hearth. She twisted around, jabbing the poker as if she would threaten the Countess herself. "The Master is good and kind and 'tis no wonder he's hardly here, now he's married to that woman." She stood up, pressed down her dress and returned to Ruth's side. "I am sorry, child – I spoke out of turn." She clasped Ruth's hand.

"You spoke nothing but the truth."

Ruth pressed her lips together, remembering an incident from years ago. Her father had stroked the side of her face, saying wistfully that she looked so like her mother. The Countess had stormed out of the room and he had been careful not to say fond words to Ruth in the woman's presence again. So much had changed. But wedlock against her will? Had her father's second marriage so dulled his heart that he would forsake his own daughter? No. She could not believe it.

"Oh Miss Ruth . . ."

"I know you will tell no-one. Promise me."

"To the grave, as ever. As I said, I cannot believe the Master would allow this. Everyone's asleep now, but if anyone asks why you were absent at supper, I'll say the skating tired you out."

"Though the Steward already knows – he was there."

Nurse rolled her eyes. "That man sticks his nose in everywhere."

"He makes everything his business. Father has let him . . . his absence."

Ruth looked down at her hands. Nurse rubbed her arm briskly. "I should fetch you a warming lemon posset."

Ruth shook her head. Food was Nurse's answer to everything.

"Shall I leave you alone, child?"

Ruth hardly heard her words. The next time she looked up Nurse had left, leaving the candle on the side cabinet. In the hallway, the timepiece struck midnight. Just a few steps along, her stepfamily slept in their bedchambers – her stepmother in her mother's room.

She recalled the first time she became aware of cruelty in her stepmother. Town gossips were saying the Countess had ordered a butcher to slaughter a puppy dog just so she could apply an infusion of puppy fat to her skin; it was thought to renew a woman's youth, though few were heartless enough to do it. The next day, Ruth found the Countess reclining in her undergarments, damp fabric smothering her face and neck. The memory turned Ruth's stomach. That was one thing, but forcing her into marriage . . . how could her father have ever chosen such a monstrous woman? Nurse was right: that must be the reason he spent so little time at home. But did he ever think of his firstborn daughter, trapped here without him?

A rhyme echoed in her head, from sunny days when she and Silas and other children sat in circles in the orchard, counting out fruit stones after gorging on plums and cherries.

What will my husband be?
Tinker, tailor, soldier, sailor, rich man, poor man, beggar man, thief.
What shall I wear?
Silk, satin, cotton, rags.
How shall I get to church?
Coach, carriage, wheelbarrow, cart.
When I shall marry?
This year, next year, sometime, never.

Ruth thumped her pillow. Marry that rich man? Never, never, never! She couldn't give up.

Silas was her love. And she was his. He had said so just hours earlier.

She climbed out of her bed, wiped her hands over her face, rearranged her hair and smoothed down her dress. Picking up the candlestick, she turned the door handle and stepped into the empty hallway.

The storm howled at the night and the wind tugged a rattling window. Ruth went to pull it shut but as she released the catch, the wind snatched it open, blowing out her candle and billowing through her dress. She reached outside for the handle and glanced upwards: the heavens were in a fury, twisting snowflakes becoming ashen shadows.

Black snow gathers in the hollow of her eyes.

Her soul shuddered.

She snapped the window shut and beat away the snowflakes on her hair, face, and arm as though they were something foul.

The storm was entombing the hall. Like wounded animals, the walls moaned as she swept down the staircase. All was dungeon-dark. Ruth rushed past paintings of generations of Henrysons, past the family library, past the armoury, past everything she was losing to Charles. As she ran through the empty dining hall, her skirt rustled the rushes on the floor. In the kitchen, the fire in the range was burning bright, piled high with logs, but no-one was there except Bess the dog asleep by the hearth. Up Ruth stepped through the narrow stairway to the servants' quarters, a place she had not been for years – not since the Countess had objected.

Light shone from under the door of the Housekeeper's room and words trickled out . . . It was the Steward! Ruth hesitated, considered turning back, but decided against it. There wasn't a moment to lose.

She came to the first bedroom along and pushed open the door just enough to see inside. Wind blew in through cracked window glass and the makeshift curtain wavered back and forth. It was the girls' room. Four of them slept head to toe on straw mats.

Nearest to her, sleeping in a small truckle bed, a cat curled at her feet, was Little Luce. She rolled over, twisting her blanket, her long pale hair caught in her mouth as she murmured in her dreams. Asleep, she looked even younger than her five years, soft-faced like a baby. Ruth's heart rushed with warmth at her innocence. She had an urge to kiss her on the forehead but, lest she wake her, stroked the cat instead. It stretched and purred at her touch.

The next room along was fusty with sleeping, snoring bodies – many folk were staying overnight instead of battling home through the storm.

She peeked into another room and winced as the door clunked against the pisspot. Two men were slumped head to toe on a straw mattress while three more slept in their overcoats.

Silas was not here.

Ruth made her way back past the Housekeeper's room, silent now, so she was even more cautious. With the sliver of light behind her and the warm glow from the kitchen below, she trod carefully on the first step of the stairs, testing for squeaks, then the second, making her way down. She stopped dead. The orange glow was suddenly blotted out. Darkness before her intensified, shadows gathering together. She felt instant terror.

Something was there, blacking out the light.

Tears pricked her eyes.

She didn't breathe, didn't move, heard her blood pounding in her ears.

Bess the dog crept into view, ears flattened, belly low, growling at the sinister blackness.

A heavy hand grabbed her shoulder. Terrified and unable even to cry out, she lost her balance and stumbled through the pitch-black darkness, down the stairs and fell to the floor.

Somebody called her name: the Steward.

"You!" Ruth's voice shook as she began to pull herself up from the ground, while Bess nuzzled her feet.

"Yes. Me."

The Steward stepped down and stood looming over her. She stumbled back and hit the floor again. Pain shot up her wrist as it took the full force of her weight.

"What do you think you're doing?"

She was too frightened and confused to answer him. What, she wondered, had that darkness been that she had felt on the stairs? Even the dog had sensed it and was staying close to her.

The Steward did not move to help her as she pulled herself upright and moved to the table, trembling as she leant against its sturdy frame. The glow from the range lit the man from behind; she could barely make out his face. She had never liked him. But alone, here, where neither of them should be at this time of night, that dislike was turning into fear.

"Apologies, Miss Ruth." His voice was thick with irony. "I didn't mean you to fall. I'd wanted to speak quietly – didn't want to wake the servants."

"You approach me in the dark and in such a manner as this!"

"You surprised me too, Miss Ruth." Words slithered from the man. "Why were you so far from your chamber?"

"And you own this place, do you now? It is I whose family own the Hall. Am I now accountable to you? I think not."

"You are young in years, Miss Ruth, and perhaps not wise to the dangers of the world."

His words faked concern. Now her eyes had adjusted, Ruth could see him more clearly. She swallowed and squared her shoulders to face him.

"I am old enough to know the ways of men, if that is your meaning." She looked him in the eyes as best she could, though he towered over her.

"But why are you here?"

"I feel unwell. I'm looking for Nurse."

A cold smile spread across his face – he did not believe a word. She remembered passing him earlier as she left the Countess. This man did not need to inflict any physical wound to hurt her. He had already caused great damage.

"I bid you good night," said Ruth and clasped her hands.

The Steward paused, as if deciding what to do, but Ruth had closed the conversation. Then he took one step backwards and gave the smallest nod.

"Until tomorrow, Miss Ruth."

12

Thieves in the Night

The snowstorm over the town of Crowbury raged on, yet there was something about this storm that worried the wildlife out of their shelters. A fox ran from its hole, glanced upwards and crept through white-smothered tree roots into the nearby field, leaving paw prints in the snow. Robins came together, took off and left. A murder of crows arose from their nests, scattering into the clouds then retreating to the trees beside the mullioned windows of Ruth's bedchamber. They jittered along the branches, cawing and confused. Falling out of the sky amidst the snowflakes were slivers of black. These black crystals fluttered around the birds' wings, settling on twigs, nests, branches. The crows shook their feathers and flew away, their cries carrying in the eerie wind. Smatterings of black continued to fall from the sky. Then a vast shape pierced the clouds over the Hall on the hill. It was a ship's hull. Heaving, with moaning shadows that followed in its wake. The ship swayed unsteadily, turning through the broiling sky towards the town, glancing off the roof of Crowbury church as more slivers fell from its hull. It surged and slowed to a stop, a mile high over the river in the depth of the valley, as if it had dropped anchor.

The townsfolk slept on, unaware that spinning around their heads were halos transmuting their hopes and dreams.

Ragged sails were curled around the ship's mast; slithering ropes were yanked through holes; a vast gangplank was rolled out. One creature of shadows leapt down the slatted boards as they were lowered down through a mile of air. It leapt ahead and bore the gangplank's whole weight while slotting the end into a mooring on the riverside, tethering it with shore lines.

Shadowy thieves loped, swaggered, crept and swarmed down. Crowbury was under siege. They scattered through the snow-covered lanes, slipping through the walls and into rooms where children, women and men slept peacefully, none the wiser.

Sleeping cats, rats and dogs stirred. Those awake cowered and froze.

One creature of darkness moved slowly through the town, carrying a sack for its plunder. This one always hunted for the most powerful dreams, the halos most radiant with hope. They were usually around the heads of the youngest sleepers. Dreams had been stolen before from many of the older ones; their halos came away with only a little resistance. Some hardly held onto hope at all.

Working alone, the shadowy dream thief moved up the track through the wood towards the Hall it had spied from the ship. It stepped into the building as though there were no wall to prevent it. Slowly, it turned its head this way and that until it felt the location of the nearest dream. It sensed something from a room down the corridor nearby.

It slipped into the room. Silas was barely asleep, leaning over a desk, head resting on his arms. His dream halo had just begun to spin, the rainbow colours not yet moving fast enough to form the white ring of dreamlight. Still, it was bright enough for stealing.

The dream thief extended one finger. Its nail scored around the inside of the halo: the first separation of the dream and the dreamer. Now it swept its dark hand through the full-coloured rainbow beam, nullifying the dream, and touching a lock of

Silas's hair. The halo blackened and crystallised. The dream thief removed it and placed it in the sack.

Hungry for more, the dream thief lifted its head and sensed the greatest dream density in the building. It moved into the deserted kitchen and headed up towards the servants' rooms. It noted the two humans awake on the narrow stairs, but knew it would be unseen, and passed straight through Ruth and the Steward. Ruth tumbled down the steps. The dream thief barely noticed the falling girl, glancing behind as he headed towards the sleepers.

Dreamlight shone through the gaps beneath all the doors. The thief observed the varying intensities and nodded when it saw brighter dreamlight leaking around the door of one room. Silently, the thief entered.

Glowing halos were spinning around the heads of four young women, crowded together on two mats. One halo after another came away with some resistance; they would have had dreams stolen before, the thief guessed, but probably just the once.

On her small truckle bed, Little Luce was murmuring in her sleep. She raised her hand to wipe away a long lock of hair caught in her mouth. The purring cat at her feet fell silent as the dream thief drew closer. It was Little Luce's dreams that the thief coveted the most, for her halo shone and radiated the brightest of them all. Red, turquoise, emerald and gold shimmered over her hair. Before moving any closer, the dream thief watched – fascinated as always – while the rainbow turned faster and faster, blending into pure white.

As it reached out a hand, poised to steal, the halo faltered in the presence of the dream thief and stopped whirling, fracturing into the spectrum of its original colours.

The thief blew on its finger and scored around the inside of the halo, causing a fissure between the girl and her hopes and dreams. Grasping the halo with both hands, the dream thief tugged once, twice. Little Luce's head and shoulders lifted as her soul tried to hold on. Finally the links were severed. The dream let the dreamer go. The halo petrified and crystallised to ashen black. The thief placed it in the sack with the other stolen dreams. It was a prize, and it was enough for one night. He would now return to the ship.

Little Luce trembled in her sleep.

Bending down low, the thief reached out a smoky hand to gently stroke her hair. Its lips briefly touched her forehead in a kiss, then whispered into her ear.

"Now, little one, sleep a dreamless sleep."

13

Darksome Words

Distant voices broke into Silas's drifting, clouded thoughts, and fell quiet – as well they might in the dead of night.

He opened his heavy eyes, raised his head from the desk and leant back on the stool as he stretched and yawned. He had hardly slept. Just for a few moments. But now he felt even more exhausted. And empty. Blank. As though there was something, some *thing*, he could not quite reach.

Running his fingers through his hair, he glanced at the book Ruth had given him. He turned another page, absent-minded, seeing but not reading the lines of inked words in the semi-darkness, lit by the dying embers of the fire. He pushed the book away and sat still, twisting the ring on his finger.

He yawned again, smelling the lavender and other hanging herbs all around him, their sweetness so at odds with his mood. If the Cook had left out some brandy, perhaps he could finish it and knock himself out. A drink would do for him what sleep could not.

He picked up the book, slung his coat and hunting bag over his shoulder and made for the kitchen. But as he entered the room, he stopped stock still.

Ruth was there, holding up a poker.

Pale, as if she had seen a ghost. Huge eyes, breathing rapidly. Had she heard some rumour about Betsy? No – she dropped the poker the moment she recognised him. Her eyes softened and she rushed towards him, flinging her arms around his chest.

"Oh Silas!" Her words were brimming with relief, love and innocence.

And *now* he felt something.

Guilt piled upon guilt.

"I-I've hardly slept – Frobisher kept me awake," he said, indicating the book in his hand, which he then put in his hunting bag. "What ails thee?"

"Hold me!" Ruth was holding back tears. She burrowed into his chest, feeling for his heartbeat. "'Tis the gravest news. The Countess intends marriage for me."

Silas squeezed her tight. He felt the bare skin of her back through her nightdress. Her fingertips were on his skin; his chest was pounding. He held her tighter still, even tighter, and let her go.

"We mustn't be caught together now," he said.

Ruth gasped. "What does it matter? My stepmother made it plain she knows about us!"

"God in heaven!"

"Silas?"

"I could be dismissed!"

Ruth blinked rapidly. "But . . . I thought . . .!"

"Ruth. They *know*! My position here hangs by a thread and you know how the Steward sees me. I'll never get a good reference. My family . . . We *can't* be found together!"

She looked astonished and gestured, spreading out her hands. "So let us run away!"

Her eyes were huge.

"No!" He took a step back.

She crumpled.

He winced – he had been too harsh. "Oh Ruth. Come with me."

He led her down the passageway, looking for somewhere they would be undisturbed, but the Steward – if he was prowling about – would hear voices from anywhere around here. Silas grabbed a cape from the hooks, draped it around her shoulders and pulled on his coat. A barrage of snow hit them as he opened the door. Without thinking, he reached for her hand and they ran to the stables.

Once inside, she opened her mouth to speak but he pressed his finger to her lips to silence her. Quickly, he made sure they were alone. He took her into the tack room and removed a saddle from a bale of hay. They both sat down.

She told him everything that had happened. But he could hardly focus on her words. This turn of events could be a convenient way out for him. Marriage to another man was not what Ruth wanted but it would solve many things. He would not have to leave Crowbury to escape having to choose between the two girls – yet could he be at peace with Betsy, knowing he had hurt Ruth? He doubted it, unless he left marrying Betsy for some time so that Ruth did not suspect betrayal – yet even this did not feel right, because something in him would not be content with a village girl. He had always yearned for a bigger life, one that he had imagined through reading all those books. Sometimes he had wondered how he could pursue his own dreams in a way that did not hurt his family.

But now he felt so confused about what he wanted.

His old dreams felt out of reach.

He had no clear sense of direction, and this worried him as much as what Ruth was sharing. All he knew was what the Steward would do if he left now with Ruth; the man had him in a stranglehold.

On she went. For Silas it was like looking into the eyes of an injured animal. He still cared for her, and could not hurt her by speaking of his confusion.

He swallowed sharply.

"Don't you see, Silas?" she was saying. "You and I could go to London tonight, to father's warehouse in Blackwall, send a message to him through his men. They will know where he is. And we could find a bookbinding apprenticeship for you."

He shifted on the bale.

She carried on. "If only he knew, father would prevent the betrothal to Boswell! We must find a way to delay it until he returns. It will be months."

Silas shook his head.

"Silas, you know father would never do anything to hurt me, but he's on the other side of the world – even further than the Balkans!"

"The Countess has timed it to perfection."

"Yes, but I am certain his men would get a letter to him."

He said nothing in reply. He knew she would be puzzled by his slowness to agree. He dropped his head into his hands.

Ruth touched his fingers. "Silas?"

He removed his hand and gestured. "We'd have no licence to travel without the Countess's say-so."

"London is only a day's ride! We could be there tomorrow if we left now!" Frustration was building in her voice.

"Ruth, that's not how it works! You are not listening. A travel licence is still needed. Without one, there's no entry through the city gates."

Still she persisted. "We could take a wherry down the Thames – you must know someone here who works on the river who could help us?"

"The plague is there . . ." He glanced at Ruth.

Her eyes narrowed. "What are you talking about, Silas? You know full well the plague has passed. I went to Whitehall just last month!"

Silas shrugged and looked at the floor.

"I thought you wanted to *leave* Crowbury!" Ruth said, looking him straight in the eyes.

She would not let him be! He stared at his boots. "My family need me," he finally mumbled.

Ruth started at his words.

"You do not understand," he blustered. "Your life has been so coddled that you can't understand the pressures I'm under. *If* I ran away with you, the Steward would make it very difficult for my family, impossibly difficult. They'd be thrown off the estate. The Countess would move heaven and earth to find you and bring you back. Whereas if I bide my time, I'd have a reference." He shifted uncomfortably on the bale.

Ruth breathed out sharply.

Silas said nothing more.

"And that is your final word?" Ruth asked.

Silas looked sheepishly at her. "What you ask of me . . ."

Ruth stood up.

"Stare at the stars too long, dear Ruth, and you'll fall in a ditch." He meant it lightly, to push her away, but the words came out cruel.

"You think me some giddy girl?"

He shook his head. "Could you not stay with Meg a while? Send your letter for help from there?"

At this Ruth laughed sharply. "But she is to be wed, too! I'd wanted to tell you, before, but . . . Oh!" Ruth's eyes flashed with anger. "Meg told me yesterday on the ice. She was quite happy, Silas! To leave her home and marry a stranger who spied her across the room!"

"She will feel 'tis a daughter's duty," Silas said, thinking of the pressures on him to do as his own family wished and marry Betsy.

Ruth recoiled. "And there we have it. That is what you think I should do. Submit myself to an old man. That woman says he will break me like one of these horses!"

Her words cut deep – he had missed so much of what she'd said! He reached for her hand. She snatched it away.

"Oh, go to your precious family!" she cried and ran out of the stables, into the swirling shadows of the storm.

14

A Spinning Circle of Light

Everywhere she turns, she sees black snow. It coats every surface, muffles every sound. Little shadows move in every direction. She listens out for the boy's cry for help: there it is – as though she is trapped in a moment she is forever destined to revisit. He is screaming now, turning to ice. "Help me! Please help me!" The freezing boy whimpers and reaches out his fingers towards her. She tries to run away from his touch but cannot: black snow holds her ankles fast and will not let go. But now there is another voice, calm, deep and honeyed – a voice she has never heard before – breaking into her dream. "Ruth. Be not afraid. Open your eyes, Ruth, open your eyes."

Ruth opened her eyes, swollen with tears.

Shining bright light! She shot up, backing away, lifting her hand to shield her eyes yet desperate to see.

The glow lessened and its source became clear.

Something was at the foot of her bed.

She rubbed her eyes.

She fought to take in an astonishing creature! She didn't know where to start. Standing strong. Muscular like a man. Yet luminous.

Her heart – so hurt – raced.

There was a robe of gleaming thread . . . dark Moorish skin with an unearthly glow like sunlight striking a raven . . . dark hair falling in coils to the shoulders . . . a spinning circle of light around his forehead – just like the halos around the heads of holy people she had seen in paintings. And angels.

She looked more closely. Surely she was dreaming? There were wings – magnificent dark-feathered wings moving gently behind him, glossy, touched here and there by the colours of emeralds and rubies. And not just two wings, but four, like some great seraph filling the room.

His expression was serious but his eyes were warm. She had the feeling that this creature was as surprised to see her as she was him . . . *if* this really was real. Looking at him felt like waking in sunshine in a meadow. Peace bubbled inside her and her earlier desperation evaporated. *Was* this a dream?

"Good eve, Ruth."

He knew her name! His voice was deep and soothing.

"My name is Godrick."

He walked around the bed, his wings rustling as he moved. His robe was woven with exotic silks of oranges, lemons, limes, and was so close she could reach out and touch its woven patterns. Her finger twitched, but she did not move. The dark skin of his arms gave off light. It was all completely unfathomable.

Godrick gently placed his hands over her head in a blessing. She knew somehow that she needn't cry out. Calmness washed over her. It was as though an invisible pebble of peace had dropped into the centre of her being, dissolving her distress.

He released his hands. As he did, Ruth could see colours moving around her forehead like a small, circular rainbow. Myriad shades of red, blue and yellow moved faster and faster, and blended to white like crushed stars. She was dreaming a hundred perfect dreams all at once, nullifying the pain in her heart. It was bliss.

He stepped well back, still charged with light.

Ruth blinked. If she closed her eyes for longer, would he disappear? The question burst out.

"You're an angel?"

"I am a messenger," he said. "A messenger who carries dreams – sent by the Guardian of Dreams when a new dream is needed."

"Guardian of Dreams?"

Godrick nodded. "Hopes and dreams are a light within and a light to guide, so precious that no soul should relinquish their dream." The messenger looked at her carefully. "Nor should any other steal another's dream."

The messenger spoke in mysteries, yet what he said felt so simple and true. But then her haunting dream came to the edge of her thoughts, and her skin prickled.

Godrick said nothing, as though waiting for her to speak.

She ventured her thoughts. "*All* dreams – does the Guardian make them all?"

Godrick looked her in the eye. "No, not all are from The Guardian of Dreams. The only way to discern this is by its fruit . . . by this I mean, how the dream prompts the soul to act, and what that leads to."

"But most of my dreams make no sense."

"Perhaps you have felt a nudge within," the messenger continued, "awakening your curiosity? Or urging you to take another path? Through your dream the Guardian plants hopes and visions deep in your soul, to a depth the waking mind cannot fathom. They manifest in ideas, impulses . . . a longing for something good. See, here, this is how they are made."

Once again, the messenger placed his hands on Ruth's head. And what she saw next felt like a dream within a dream.

A tree stretches high, covered with waxy dew-laden leaves and fruits weighing down the branches. The trunk is knotted and broad with intricate ridges of bark – so full of colour! Not just brown but a little green here, lilac there, rust there – so full of life! Around her, long grasses sway, dotted with poppies, daisies, blue-bells. There's a large, dark pool of water, a spring bubbling at the far end, ripples reaching across. Coming into her view on the opposite bank is blazing light in the shape of a figure, walking. He – or she – is kneeling before the pool. So bright is this light that Ruth wants to step backwards, as though she were actually there, and momentarily opens her eyes. There is a spinning white halo. Godrick's hands are still raised above her head. She closes her eyes again.

The figure is infinitesimally infused with light, even more than Godrick when he first appeared. Who is this? The Guardian of Dreams? On its head is a pointed crown of light. Each point rises high, quivering as though made of a golden flame.

Ruth sees into the pool now, yet after that blinding brightness there is only darkness. One by one, scattered specks of light appear, as though the surface of the pool is not a reflection but a moving picture. The specks grow and grow until they resemble stars and planets . . . the heavenly globes, as though their Armillary Sphere is bursting into life. Now water droplets arise from the pool, gathering together to form a misty impression of a girl, surrounded now by a blur of pictures like a moving tapes-try. Still glowing, the Guardian's hands are at work, moving slowly and gently within the blur. Once again, a band of water droplets arise – this time forming a halo around the girl's head. A beam of light streams out towards the halo from the Guardian's fingertips! The whiteness splits into different colours and spins and spins around her head. She lifts her eyes and smiles. Then her watery figure disappears, leaving the rainbow halo. A dream.

15

A Thread to Follow

Thunder rumbled and crackled in the distance. Ruth woke. It was morning. The room was empty.

She lay still, looking at the stitches on the canopy above her bed. She screwed up her eyes. Nothing made sense anymore. So much ran through her mind. Her stepmother's eyes . . . Boswell's portrait . . . Meg's marriage . . . Silas pulling his hand out of hers . . . and now that curious 'messenger' who called himself Godrick . . . they had spoken, hadn't they? But surely that angel had been her imagination at work when she was sleeping.

She reached over and pulled back the thick curtain from the mullioned window. Daylight flooded in. Rain trickled down the tiles, melting the snow. A heavy mist hid the horizon as though the sky had folded in on itself.

She would not know what to do or say when she next saw the Countess, or anyone else. Her chest felt tight.

But she had to do something – she had to get out of the Hall.

Her dress was still damp from running through the stormy courtyard with Silas, but not wanting to delay even one minute, she did not change into fresh clothes. She grabbed a cape from her cupboard, fastened it around her neck and took the bread Nurse had left.

Very quietly, she opened the door and listened out for the Countess. There was no noise, save for the ticking of the clock.

Its hands stood almost at eleven: she had slept so deeply! No-one had missed her at breakfast and thought to awaken her – not even Anna, who would usually burst in to play when she was slow to come downstairs.

For once, as Ruth made her way down towards the front door, she was hardly aware of the servants as they stoked fires and passed by, carrying bundles of sheets. The household was unusually muted. They greeted Ruth but she looked at no-one, avoiding conversation – and also gossip, for her eyes still felt swollen from tears.

As she passed by the dining-room, Bess bounded over and nuzzled into her hand, but Ruth could not take comfort from it, remembering how the dog, too, had sensed the devilish darkness on the kitchen stairs the night before. Had that really been last night?

And now she heard the Countess. The woman's voice rang out from the kitchen as she bellowed at the servants. Ruth stiffened and bolted for the main door, passing Little Luce standing quietly. Something made her stop and look back. She tried to catch Little Luce's eye but she was downcast, her face to the floor.

Ruth had never seen the child simply standing still before. Perhaps she had been rebuked by her father?

Yet something felt unnatural.

She looked different, like a child from the poor house, a shadow of herself.

Ruth wanted to go and ask her what was wrong, but the Countess's voice reached her once more from the kitchen. She needed to get away from the Hall, from Silas, from all of this. So she closed her heart to her little friend, turned away and slipped outside. She pushed the door firmly shut and leant back on its iron studs.

The courtyard was quiet. Two stable-boys led horses through the slush towards the carriage house. No Silas. No sign of the

Steward. She let out a sigh. The air was fresh and she drank it in. A fine mist of rain refreshed her skin. Lifting her hood, she headed for the path through the wood. It was all so quiet, as though the world was holding its breath. She reached out for branches to steady herself as she made her way down the slippery path.

Her thoughts swarmed. It was hard to comprehend what was taking place. The Countess casting her out of her own home! The contrast with her mother could not be sharper. Even this very track held loving memories . . . so many winters ago, snow creaking under their feet as Ruth had looked up at her mother's face, watching her lips as she spoke softly, her hand engulfed by her mother's own. Mother had compared the trees' fine filigree branches to lace, and the stream's frozen waterfall to Venetian glass. They had thrown skidding pebbles that whistled along winding ribbons of ice, and as light left the sky they pointed to the full moon behind the trees and watched clouds slide past slowly, like ships on a sea.

Suddenly it was not her mother's hand she pictured holding her own, but Silas's.

She stopped and grabbed the nearest branch, feeling dizzy.

Rain was splattering on her cape, heavier now. Fingers of water slid down the inside of her hood. Wisps of hair stuck to her face. Her feet were sodden.

She pressed on. At last she reached Crowbury's graveyard. It looked deserted. The path to the church was just as treacherous with slush. Off it, two dogs, mad with hunger, were digging around for bones and small animals. Reaching the covered entrance, she leant against the wall, catching her breath, and ate the bread, glad for it. She wiped the crumbs from her mouth and wrung out the bottom of her cape.

The church door was not quite closed and she gently pushed it open. And stopped dead.

Half the roof had caved in with the storm.

Tiles and splinters were strewn everywhere. A roof beam had smashed into the simple altar, breaking off one edge of stone. Rain was hammering down on pews covered with leaves, shards of plaster and detritus blowing in from the wood.

At the head of the church, a great yew, felled by the wind, speared the window, its broken green arm punching the air.

She made straight for the family vault and swept away leaves, muddy beechnuts, pine needles, grit. Underneath, the surface was still solid. She fell to her knees, rain beating down upon her from the open sky. Soaking, she reached out for the curve of letters that spelt her mother's name on the side of the tomb.

Her heart ached.

She pressed her hands against the cold, wet stone – the closest she could ever be to her – and suddenly saw her hands as though for the first time, feeling that everything was being swept away through her fingers. She could grip onto nothing, stop nothing from being lost to her. Her old life, so carefree, was folded up like a blanket, put away out of reach.

"Mama," Ruth said aloud, the word carried away by the wind.

Father had held her so tight during the funeral . . . but where was he now?

She remembered the weave of his coat pressed against her cheek as he squeezed her even tighter while stone scraped against stone, sealing her mother's body inside the vault. Ruth had not understood then that they would be forever separated. Her fingers pressed even tighter into the stone with the memory, and she released them.

Ruth sat in one of the sodden pews. It felt like madness . . . the Countess . . . Silas . . . the dream of black snow and a freezing boy . . . and now the angel in her room. Angel? She rubbed her face. Had that 'messenger' really been a dream? Her spirit had lifted, and could that really have come from within her when she was feeling so upset, when everything was so lost?

A sudden change in the light caught her eye. Sun had broken through a cloud and shone through a high, small stained-glass window – one of the few remaining – casting coloured shafts of light that fell to the floor. She steadied her breaths. She felt drawn to go and stand and bathe in its light, but did not move.

It was such a distinct beam. Beautiful, like a rainbow, in the midst of this bedlam.

And as she watched the beam of light, something lit up in her mind.

She knelt down once again, examining the carving on her mother's tomb.

Yes: a rainbow! Ruth imagined it continuing on and plunging into the darkness of Earth and round to meet its other side, completing a circle. Last night – whether she had dreamt it or not – when the messenger placed his hands on her head, she had seen colours moving around like a tiny rainbow! It was the same with the vision. The Guardian of Dreams had created a dream halo for the girl hovering above the pool: a rainbow spinning in a never-ending circle.

"*Non Sine Sole Iris,*" whispered Ruth, "No Rainbow Without Sun."

She stood up, drops of rain falling relentlessly around her.

Her parents had always encouraged her to hold onto her hopes and dreams, every time they said bedtime prayers with her. Her heart beat faster. She knew that rainbows were an ancient symbol of hope, a place where dark storms were touched by light . . . all these rainbows must surely speak of darkness being touched by hope – and by dreams.

16

Hearth and Heart

Breathless, Ruth slipped into Crowbury Hall and listened out for the Countess. She nodded to the servant who was turning rushes on the floor of the dining-room and made for the kitchen. The door was ajar. She could not hear her stepmother's voice.

Nurse and Cook huddled together on the bench, talking in subdued tones. As Ruth walked in, Nurse looked up, her face already creased in a frown.

"Miss Ruth!" Nurse rushed to greet her while Cook picked up a carrot from the table behind her and began to strip its skin. "Dear, your clothes are wringing wet!" Nurse fussed, taking off Ruth's cape and hanging it up beside the range to dry.

"Is she here?" Ruth asked in a low voice, before she could say anything else.

Nurse dropped her voice too. "No. Don't fret, Miss – they're taking Charles back to Oxford, then on to Little Appleton for the night."

A day's grace, Ruth thought. "The church . . . do you know what happened?"

Cook looked over sharply. "No?"

"The roof fell in with the storm."

"I must fetch the Steward!"

Ruth tensed. "Not yet. Please!" She needed to be able to breathe.

Cook looked over to Nurse, who nodded. Cook raised an eyebrow but stayed where she was, pulling the knife down over the carrot.

"It is all such a mess. It's sad." Ruth meant more than just the church. But how could she talk about what was happening? She barely understood it herself. She shivered and rubbed her hands in front of the fire.

Nurse smiled in sympathy and dipped a ladle into a pot. "Here, take some broth." She placed the steaming bowl at a space on the table.

Just the scent of rosemary and meat revived Ruth. She swung her legs over the bench, pulled a chunk of bread off a loaf and dipped it into the broth, but Nurse touched her hand, reminding her of her manners. Which, given the gravity of everything that was happening, cheered Ruth up.

"Bless thy gifts," she murmured. It tasted good. She ate quickly, feeling hungrier with every mouthful, while the two women busied themselves with tasks.

Before she finished, one of the maids burst into the kitchen from the pantry, red-faced and excited.

"And there's more!" Sarah announced to Nurse and Cook. "The butcher just came up here and I overheard him telling the Steward about his sister and his nieces and nephews – all silent and strange and sad, not saying a word, too . . ."

"Sarah . . ." Cook's voice was full of warning.

"What now?" asked Ruth.

"Well, all that crying in the night here," said Sarah turning to Ruth, regardless. "Little Luce being like a meek lamb this morning and not saying boo to a goose, then sobbing without ceasing, so she's been carried down to her aunt's." Sarah was gabbling, her eyes gleaming with the gossip.

Ruth's hand hovered with her spoon.

"And that's not all, 'cos the potter's wife and his two young 'uns, everyone's saying they're not themselves, and the blacksmith's lad's gone last night! Proper gone! Snatched or summat!"

"Gone?" Ruth asked, putting down her spoon.

"Sarah, that's quite enough," said Nurse sharply. "Miss Ruth needn't be worried by tittle-tattle."

"Go ask the Housekeeper what needs to be done next," said Cook.

Ruth looked at the two women as the girl climbed the stairs.

"How very strange indeed," she said.

"'Tis the time of year," said Nurse, her curls shaking. "We could help with herbs from the Still Room?"

Nurse looked like she needed a bit of calming chamomile herself, Ruth thought.

"Of course, yes. But the missing blacksmith's lad . . . has the Justice of the Peace been informed?"

"I believe they've done so," said Cook.

Ruth shook her head. "We should all say prayers tonight . . ."

"We shall be doing that," said Cook solemnly.

"Poor Little Luce," said Ruth, taking a last mouthful. She pictured her standing so still in the dining-room and felt full of regret for not going to her. "I saw her, this morning. She did not look herself."

"Don't fret about her, Miss Ruth."

They were trying to reassure her, but still Ruth felt concerned. At least, with the Countess away for one night, she had a little time to herself. She dabbed the corners of her mouth, swung her legs back over the bench and jumped up.

"Heavens, girl! Will you not settle? You'll make yourself ill!"

"I shall be back for supper," Ruth called out behind her. "There's somewhere I must go."

She ran down the passageway and was grabbing a dry coat and a riding crop as Nurse caught up with her.

"Miss Ruth," Nurse whispered. "That Lord . . . the one, you know . . . he's coming here tomorrow."

Boswell, coming to claim her.

Ruth paused, then continued to pull her arms through the coat and button it through.

"We've been told to prepare the house and make ready."

17

A Fault Line

The road was treacherous but Ruth flicked her horse's reins, urging him on as his hooves dented the slush. She wanted to gallop, desperate to find a way to escape the Countess's trap. Tomorrow everything would change. Lord Boswell was coming and there was nothing she could do to stop that.

"Go on, go on, good boy."

She pressed in her heels and flicked the reins hard, forcing the horse to pick up speed. He tossed his mane and snorted hot breath into the freezing air as though breathing out fire.

Silas had been in the tack room. Her stomach had flipped over when he moved away without so much as a glance, his head hung low like a beaten dog. Pain had gripped her heart and lingered. But this was not the Silas she thought she knew. Her respect for him was beginning to ebb away, though even this was painful. She shut her eyes tight for a moment and held her breath. Opening them, she reached out for the horse's mane as if for the comfort of touching another living thing, and noticed her sleeve: in the dank air her clothes were already pearled with moisture, like little tears.

The midwinter light was already on the turn when she reached her father's warehouse on the outskirts of Crowbury, housed in what remained of the old monastery. Father had re-roofed it to hold his salt, pitch and timber imports from the Balkans for selling throughout the county. She dismounted and led the horse up the pathway to the door around the side. She banged her fist on it. A worker she did not recognise answered.

"Can I speak with Mr Tanner?"

"He's not here, Miss."

"His foreman?"

"Neither Miss, down in Blackwall just now."

She looked beyond to the stacks of crates inside – there were fewer men there than usual, and nobody she knew. If there had been, she could have sent a direct message to her father. As it was, any letter she sent through Crowbury would be intercepted by the Steward. She was sure of it. As Crowbury Hall's manager and rent-collector the Steward knew everybody, and had their respect – or fear.

She had to find another way to reach her father.

She turned her horse around, and they walked together back up the pathway, joining the road which was busier now with workers coming home for the night. She mounted and nudged the horse onwards, needing to make quick progress, but the horse was still hesitant. Meg was probably the only person who could help – just as Silas had suggested last night. Silas . . . He had been so altered, so painfully different . . . rejecting her only hours after he spoke of a future together. She found her hand was gripping the whip so tight, her knuckles whitened. She cracked it against the horse's side and could not stop herself crying out.

At that moment, the horse's hoof slid and gave way. One of the men passing on the road leapt forwards and grabbed the bridle.

"There now, hush, steady now," the man said, two sweeps of his hand helping to calm the horse.

"Thank you!" said Ruth, patting the horse's neck and managing to throw a brief smile of relief at the stranger.

His eyes twinkled and he smiled boldly – as though he knew her, which felt a little impudent to Ruth. Had he been at the feast? Not dressed in those old-fashioned clothes, for she would have remembered. He wore a square lace collar over a short cape, striped breeches and a tall wide-brimmed hat, which he lifted as a mark of respect. It could be the costume of a street player, but he was not dishevelled, as she would have expected.

"Take care when making haste, gentle lady." His look was as pointed as a quill pressing into paper.

She bristled.

"It would," he continued, "do no good to go breaking your horse's leg." He was holding on too long to the horse's reins.

This annoyed Ruth. She knew he was right – it was hardly the first time she had been berated for being impetuous. But what else was she to do when so much was at stake? And who did he think he was, saying that to her? She did not respond other than nod politely, and continued on her way, leaving Crowbury behind as quickly as she could.

She could have walked beside the horse instead of riding, but that would have taken too long, and besides, the snow was more compact here, safer than slush.

Field workers walked back past her towards the town, collars lifted against the cold. Cattle huddled together at the edges of the fields. She took the left track at the crossroads, which she recognised thanks to the clutch of draughty-looking cottages, and then, soon after, turned right. The journey was feeling longer than by coach, so she dug in her heels and the horse picked up pace. It hesitated, passing a group of startled young deer that dived away into the thickening mist. Ruth urged the beast onwards. The deer park meant she was almost there.

Ruth wondered what her grandfather would have made of her – surely he would approve of her courage, her determination?

Her mother had read to her from his journals, and in recent years, Ruth had read them for herself. His stories were not always about exotic discoveries and beautiful landscapes – he also told of events that touched and troubled him.

One such account related to a night at Crowbury Hall when the Armillary Sphere, days off the boat from Italy, had been presented at a feast. How life could turn on a pinhead for evil or for good . . . On that night, Richard had taken it upon himself to protect his younger sister Mary from an older suitor who was none other than their guest, King Henry the Eighth. It was the incident that the Countess had mentioned the day before. Ruth squeezed her heels into the horse's side at the memory. The King's fifth wife had been beheaded for adultery – hardly the first wife he'd had killed – and it was well known that he was minded to take a new woman. The King's lascivious remarks about Mary had so worried Richard that he discreetly kept his sister away from the feast – away from the King's gaze. It worked. The King looked elsewhere and married another girl, Katherine Parr, months later.

Yet in protecting his sister, Richard felt he had forsaken his young friend, the son of that candle-maker. Ruth had found it difficult to decipher what had happened at the feast, but the young lad's Master Curiosity presentation to the King was a disaster, despite their good rehearsals. In the journals, Richard expressed great sorrow that he had not been present to intervene. Despite searching everywhere, he never saw the boy again and blamed himself for his disappearance. He felt responsible.

It was a story to which Ruth had returned more than once because it told her so much about her grandfather's kindness and the way he lived his life. She was sure that, had he lived long enough to meet her, he would have been appalled by the Countess, acting like this in his dead daughter's shoes.

Ruth was chilled to her very bones. The mist thickened in the falling darkness. Time was not on her side.

At last the elegant outline of Meg's house emerged, a welcome sight. The footman took her horse as Ruth rushed in, calling for her friend. Meg swept down the staircase, grabbed Ruth's hands and kissed her brightly on both cheeks.

"Dear friend!" Ruth felt a rush of warmth for Meg and was engulfed by a sense of relief that all felt well between them.

"Ruth, you are so cold! And why do you wear this old thing?"

Ruth had forgotten she had taken one of the servant's coats. Meg pulled her into a side room, helped to remove the coat and hung it up beside the fire with a dainty shake, scattering the beads of damp.

"You look well!" Ruth said, suddenly noting the way Meg's eyes shone. She touched the pale blue silk embroidery on the sleeve of Meg's new dress. "This becomes you."

"Thank you," said Meg as they sat down beside the fireplace. "It hides the bruise from skating!"

Ruth laughed, thankful to be with her friend.

Meg leant in. "Ruth, the man to whom I am to be betrothed is here!"

Ruth's heart skipped a beat. She thought of Boswell, who would have already started his journey to Crowbury from Cheshire.

"Our parents wanted us to meet to make sure I was content. I have little time to speak, I must get back to them – his parents are here, too, but it is all good news!" Meg, already subtle in her tones, lowered her voice even more, and spoke quickly. "He is a pleasant, reasonable kind of man. Quietly spoken."

"You like him?"

"Yes, I do."

Ruth's eyes filled with tears as Boswell's portrait came to mind. "I am glad for you Meg – and I am so sorry for my words yesterday."

"Yes, I was a little surprised."

"I will miss you, Meg. That's the truth."

"Yes, of course, and I will miss you too, but don't worry, we will see each other again – often! I will make sure of it."

Ruth shook her head as if to dismiss Meg's reassurance. "What is his age?"

Meg looked startled by the urgency in her voice. "I know not, perhaps eight years more than you and I. But why does this make you look even more sad?" Meg smiled, willing Ruth to be happy for her.

Ruth nodded and paused. "'Tis . . . well I am glad for you Meg, but . . . I know not how to tell you, but the strangest things have been taking place . . . My stepmother has planned marriage for me."

"Oh, I can see it will be hard to stop things with Silas . . ."

Ruth waved a hand in dismissal. How could she even begin to explain what had happened with Silas? But that was not the half of it.

"But just think – we will both be married. It is exciting!"

Ruth shook her head. "Meg, he is old – older than father! She tells me he is cruel!"

Meg's eyes widened. "Cruel? But then why would she arrange this? It makes no sense."

"You know she has always resented me. This man fits her wishes perfectly."

Meg touched Ruth's arm. "Perhaps you misheard her? Do not think so poorly of her, Ruth. It was hard for her to follow your dear mama. It would be hard for anyone."

Ruth put her hand over Meg's, squeezing tight. "I heard all too well. Meg, please permit yourself some criticism of her in my defence!"

"And you share your mother's beauty! You will be a constant reminder of what the Earl has lost, especially now you have become a young woman – oh that surprises you, Ruth! Did you not realise how similar you look? That portrait of her . . ."

Ruth shook her head. "Even supposing I did share her beauty, it does not justify this."

"Of course, but surely your stepmother did not *truly* mean to say that he is cruel!?"

"You have to believe it! She enjoyed telling me! She was smiling!"

Meg touched her lip with a finger, glancing downwards. She said nothing.

"You do not believe me?"

"It is not that – more that I know my own parents would only entrust me to a man whom they believed to be good, as good as they are."

Ruth stiffened.

"Oh my friend," said Meg gently.

"You spoke the truth for yourself, Meg, but my stepmother *has* always resented me and I believe she has arranged this when father was away – precisely for that reason, because he would never approve such a match."

"I see."

"I fear she will try to force matters soon. She has said as much."

"Yes, perhaps." Meg thought for a moment, and then whispered. "It was, apparently, the Countess's idea for us to go to Court to watch the play last month. It was she who contacted my aunt. When mother told me yesterday, I did find that a little strange."

Ruth sat back, shocked. She had been so grateful to visit London again and had been so enraptured by the play that she had been blind to the Countess's plot. She felt sick to her stomach now she understood that as she was bewitched by the story of love lost and found, her own marriage was being arranged. Boswell had no doubt spied her in the audience and marked her out as a wife.

She couldn't speak.

"Surely, dearest Ruth, she would mean you no harm! Who would?"

Ruth looked down at her hands. "When you have experienced nothing but love, Meg, it is hard for you to imagine anyone being capable of cruelty."

"All I mean is that perhaps it is not as bleak as you imagine. Perhaps Lord Boswell is not cruel, but wise? A fatherly figure of a husband for you?"

"You would rather believe that, than what I have told you?"

"I think perhaps you could make an effort to . . . How can I say this? . . . Perhaps the pleasure you would give in submitting to their wishes would give you some satisfaction in return."

Ruth stared at her friend, her eyebrows raised. It was as if they had shared nothing in all these years.

"No?"

"No!" Ruth replied, pressing her nail in so hard into the chair, she marked the wood.

They sat in silence. Ruth could think of nothing to say that would not show her anger or humiliate Meg. Her criticism of yesterday came to mind, 'a doll with an empty head'; now it did not feel so far from the truth.

"I came here," Ruth said at last, "to apologise for my sharpness yesterday, and to ask if – if I might stay with your aunt in London until father returns. I need to go straightaway."

"Oh!" Meg turned her face away and looked into the fire.

Ruth continued quickly. "It would make it more difficult for the Countess to force me into the marriage. I would need to ask for a coach, and for your parents to obtain a travel licence from the bailiff, and it would need to happen quickly, tonight, before the Countess returns from Oxford tomorrow – she's bringing Lord Boswell to meet me . . ." Ruth caught her breath. "I'd need to borrow a few things, as I fear the Steward would not let me go again if he suspects anything. I understand this is much to ask, Meg, but I thought it was better than ask to stay with you because this is the first place the Countess would think of . . . there would be a scene. I wanted to spare your family the embarrassment . . ."

Even as Ruth spoke, she saw how far-fetched her idea was, and her voice tailed away.

Meg's eyes were still fixed on the fire.

At last she turned to Ruth with her face pulled into a sympathetic smile. "The whole matter is vexing, dearest Ruth, but my aunt does not like scandal, particularly not so close to Court. I know she would not bear it."

Before Ruth could respond, there was a knock at the door and one of the housemaids entered. Meg's mother was eager for her daughter to rejoin their guests. Meg nodded, assuring the maid that she would return presently.

"Could not your cousins in the North be of help?" Meg added, as soon as the door was shut.

Ruth brightened. "We last met three years ago, perhaps . . . they live in York so I would still need your help with transport and a licence, else I cannot leave the area."

Meg took Ruth's hands in her own. "My dear friend, I fear my parents would not countenance it. They would consider it improper to go against the Countess."

Ruth breathed out abruptly. She moved and crouched down beside the fire, seized the poker and stabbed at the logs, blinking back her tears. "But my father would thank them for it," she said at last.

"They would feel it is too great a risk, choosing your father over the Countess – even supposing that he would go against his wife and oppose the marriage!"

Ruth tutted. "Of course he would! Could you not even ask them?"

"Not with my guests here. They would find out and I do not want anything to mar this evening . . ."

Ruth turned to look sharply at Meg, who would not meet her eyes.

"But your mother was friends with my own! We first met as babies . . ." Ruth's voice trailed away.

Meg shifted around in her seat, rearranged her silks, tapped her finger on the arm of the chair.

Ruth took a breath and spoke again. "Could I write a letter here, now, quickly, to my father? It would only take a minute. You could send a man you trust to his London warehouse."

"Ruth, my parents would find out, with a servant gone. They would think it seditious. Could not anyone at the Hall help? Surely Silas?"

Ruth's face burned as she turned back to the fire. "They are all too scared of the Steward. And I cannot count on Silas . . ."

"Oh? But Silas has been close to you for so long! How sad."

Ruth shot her a look. "Precisely."

Disconcerted, Meg jumped up and fussed with her skirts. "Dear thing, I want to stay, I really do, but I must go – Mama is not happy."

Ruth stood. In comparison, Meg's life, which she had derided only the day before, was so protected. She could not possibly understand Ruth's pain.

"Why is your mother unhappy? I would have thought she would be overjoyed tonight."

"Oh, she is happy enough in that way. It is the staff. They were all slow to arrive this morning from the town. They were late with lunch, out of sorts and distracted, and one of the children was making a frightful noise."

Ruth remembered Little Luce, and Sarah's comments. "I heard of strangeness in Crowbury, too."

"Some winter illness . . ." Meg nodded to the maid who popped her head around the door. "I must go, dearest."

Ruth took the coat from its hook and pulled it on. "Well. Go to your mother – and your husband."

"Not my husband yet," said Meg lowering her eyes, missing Ruth's edge of sarcasm.

18

Revelation

Ruth urged the horse across the field, still shivering with shock as much as the cold. Meg, her oldest friend, refused to help. A fissure had opened wide between them. Ruth had never felt more alone.

The horse tossed his head, struggling to step through the sodden soil. Ten minutes previously, she had turned across the ditch to take a shortcut home, but now the gathering darkening fog was concealing landmarks along the way. The colder air was sharp against her skin. Fresh ice was forming over snowmelt. It was treacherous.

She sat up straighter in the saddle; the leather creaked in the silence.

"*Non Sine Sole Iris*." Ruth spoke out aloud, slowly, feeling every word in her mouth, her breath misting in the dank air. *No Rainbow Without Sun.*

The first time she had read that phrase was the year before. It was inscribed on a painting hanging at White Hall Palace. Her step had slowed as she looked at this vast portrait of Queen Elizabeth holding a rainbow in her right hand, with those Latin words carefully painted above the little bow. Moments later, she had caught up with Meg and her aunt as they turned into the Royal Chamber, where everything revolved around the woman at the centre – God's Sovereign, who led the country alone in hope and determination. The fierce strength of the woman's eyes was admirable, and the way she commanded the Court around her.

Now, as Ruth's horse stepped unsteadily through the snowy clods, it struck her how the Queen also defied pressures from all quarters to marry. She had heard it spoken of, but had never really considered it before.

Ruth looked around. No shapes of trees or distant buildings were visible in the thickening fog. The horse sensed her fear, stamped and snorted. She kicked him onwards and they picked their way through.

Just in time, Ruth dodged a low branch that emerged suddenly through the fog. They stepped forwards again. Branches came at her from every corner, spearing the dank air.

She slid down from her saddle, took the bridle and led the horse on, reaching out with her hands to keep them both safe, hoping this was the edge of Crowbury Wood. She stumbled over the tangle of mossy undulations and roots, tearing her dress as she fell.

Clambering to her feet, rubbing her hands, she paused. All of a sudden, she felt a presence. Somebody was there, to her right. She was sure of it.

"Hello?"

Her insides felt liquid with fear. Was it the same devilish blackness she had sensed on the stairs the night before? If that had just been her imagination, the dog would not have reacted too, baring its teeth and growling.

Turning back, going in any other direction, would solve nothing. There was no other place to go. She tugged the horse's reins to the left and stepped onwards, feeling uneasy, leading the horse uphill through the trees, ducking, dodging, looking behind her. The horse's ears were twitching back and forth and Ruth patted him between the eyes – there was a film of sweat beneath her palm and it was not from exertion. Above the sound of his fearful snorts, Ruth paused every few yards, listening out for the snap of a twig, a footstep squelching . . . but there was nothing.

In time, the trees thinned and parted. The orchard wall of Crowbury Hall emerged through the fog. She let out a quick breath.

Placing one foot in the stirrup, she hitched herself up onto the saddle and rode down the pathway between fruit trees to the rear of the stables. As one fear left, another came, for she knew she was returning to her stepmother's trap.

They turned the corner.

The horse reared up, his hooves pawing the air, as Ruth struggled to stay in the saddle. Cowering beneath the hooves was that girl, Betsy.

Immediately, Ruth slid down and dismounted, apologising profusely while trying to calm her horse. Betsy leant back against the wall in a near faint, one hand to her hip, the other to her heart – even in this weather the girl's cloak was wide open, revealing the sweep of her breasts above her bodice.

"'Tis nothing Miss Ruth," Betsy replied, though her red lips and cheeks were flushed against the whiteness of her skin.

"You are not injured?"

Betsy shook her head.

As Ruth stroked and reassured her horse, she asked after the girl's stepmother, Silas's aunt.

Betsy shrugged, glanced at the ground and then looked Ruth carefully in the eyes.

"I'm blessed with Silas's help – couldn't cope without him."

Ruth's hand froze, and her heart turned over; it was the last thing she expected the girl to say.

Betsy smiled coyly, and added, "He cares very much." The girl was studying her for a reaction.

"Oh!" Ruth was too shocked to be more guarded.

"Yes, he says he does. Very much."

For a few moments, each girl held the other's stare. As Ruth looked into these knowing blue eyes, her confusion about Silas vanished. She looked away. So Betsy knew of the secret attachment between Silas and herself – and the girl was trouncing it with a secret of her own.

It was a kick in the stomach.

All had become clear. Ruth had told herself that Silas and Betsy were related, that there would be nothing between them. But, of course, they were not blood relations. There would be no impediment.

She found her breath. "I am . . . glad . . . glad to hear of it, Betsy. He speaks well of you."

Betsy's pretty lips turned up a fraction at the corners and she smiled as though shy, but she was as sly as a fox. And this coy smile was exactly how she would be drawing Silas in. Ruth realised the battle he would have been having within himself. Her heart raced.

"I was returning the hunting bag to him. See, he called by earlier with rabbit and hare for the week."

Ruth remained silent, though everything within her was screaming.

"Miss Ruth, he asked Cook to take herbs from the Still Room for my stepmother, and gave them to me himself. I hope that is acceptable?"

Ruth raised her chin and held Betsy's gaze as pain tore through her.

At last Ruth spoke.

"Of course – you take whatever you need."

19

Unmasked, Undone

Silas folded the hunting bag in two and placed it on the table. Betsy's scent lingered. She would find any excuse to see him. This time, it was returning his bag to the Hall. He had pulled her into the larder to avoid Nurse's critical eye.

He spread out his hands on the leather, rubbed his eyes and sat down heavily on the stool. Inside, he felt a dead weight. He yawned and stretched. Above him, game hung by the neck from hooks on the ceiling, ready to be butchered.

He closed his eyes and rested his head on his hands, his thoughts churning. The previous night he had not slept much at all, and now he felt sketchy and confused, as though sense and something else were just out of reach. He did not know what he wanted any more, and did not know where he was heading.

Just as his thoughts dispersed and he began to drift towards sleep, the door creaked. He heard breathing and wondered if Betsy had returned. But the breaths came sharp and hard. He heard his name being shouted across the room. And in that one word, said in that way, he knew it was Ruth, and he knew that she knew.

He jerked his head up and saw her there, her eyes blazing in the half-light. He jumped up from the stool and knocked it over.

"Ruth . . ."

"You LIAR!"

He had never seen her so angry, and it was all because of him. He reached out for her, but she sprang away.

"Don't you dare!" Ruth clenched her fists at her side, bending at the waist as though he had struck her in the stomach. "You never touch me again!"

Never before had she behaved like this. So angry, she looked like she could gut him with his own knife.

"I . . . I am sorry." He gestured, palms out.

"You cheat! And you spoke of marriage!"

"I'm sorry. I was confused . . . am . . ."

"*She* is why you did not want to run away with me!" Ruth said this even louder.

"Shhh! We must not be overheard."

At this, Ruth laughed, though her eyes were filled with tears, and she lifted one hand to her forehead in angry despair.

Silas could not look at her any more and glanced down at his feet.

"I met Betsy outside," she continued, "if you have not gathered by now. Looking the lover. Playing me for a fool."

Silas nodded, his head still low.

"You shouldn't have . . . you should have told me!"

She made for the door but he grabbed her by the wrist. She shook his hand away, disgusted.

"But I thought telling you would hurt you more," he said.

"As if I would never find out!"

"Things are not as they seem . . ."

"Betsy made it plain to me."

"Ruth, you do not understand-"

"I understand plain enough."

"No, you do not. I am not – uh – settled on Betsy."

"You think you still have a choice?!" Her outrage was growing.

"That was not my meaning. Every week my family have

pressed me to marry Betsy, and I know that she would have me, and I was thinking on it, but now I am not so sure . . ."

Ruth shook her head. "It suited you that we were a secret to your family. They knew nothing of . . . of us. You told me your heart was true, when all along . . ."

"Ruth . . . I did not mean to . . ."

"To betray me. But you did."

Yes, he felt terrible guilt now that Ruth knew the truth. But he also felt a strange relief, as though great pressure had lifted. He rolled his shoulders. No longer would he have to pretend to anyone. He breathed deeply. And Betsy was not a woman he could trust, that much was plain. He could never be content with her, given that she had divulged their secret to Ruth. He thought of his cousin Tom, whom he had also seen talk to Betsy. He would do. How had he not thought of Tom before? He was a little older, too. Betsy would like that.

"You are not the Silas I thought you were."

Her words broke into his thoughts, and he nodded. "I am not, Ruth. There are ways in which you can't know me, *never* know me, because you don't know what it is like for the rest of us when it's hard to survive. Your life is full of plenty."

"And you don't know what it's like for me," she snapped back. "I've also lost a mother, like Betsy. But she has your whole family looking out for her. I have no-one here who can protect me!" Her voice rose to a scream. "No-one!"

Silas nodded, seeing her situation afresh, and again felt the pain of betraying her. For a moment he felt a coward's shame – and this made him angry. It was not his fault that the Countess was cruel.

Ruth was reading his face. She shook her head at him and left the room, leaving the door wide open – and there was the Steward.

"You!" she shouted. Absurdly, the Steward nodded as if in deference – ridiculous, given that he was eavesdropping.

He entered the larder, a cold smirk on his face, and cracked his knuckles. "Time to go, Silas."

He left him, triumphant.

Anger surged in Silas. His eyes rose to the dead creatures hanging above, and he punched a pheasant. Feathers bloomed in the air and fell all around him like strange snow as he gathered his things together.

20

Once Seen, Never Unknown

Black crystals swirl, a furious cloud of shadows. She waits for the boy's cry for help: there it is. She follows the cries until she sees his faint outline through the shadows. "Help me, please help me," he whimpers. He reaches out his icy hand and frozen fingers grab her, the threads of his hazel eyes blackening.

Ruth opened her eyes.

Fear tore through her.

Black eyes were staring down into her own. Stinking breath swept over her face.

She blinked.

The eyes flinched, grew wider.

She couldn't swallow. Couldn't breathe, helpless beneath her bedcover.

The eyes left her own and ran up to her hair and around, scrutinising her face. Ruth glimpsed the head, neck and body stooping over her, in such shadow she could hardly see.

Tears welled and spilled over her eyelashes. The creature drew even nearer, watching closely. A smoky finger with a curled black nail like a claw reached out, as if to catch a teardrop, but hesitated as it ran down her cheek to her ear.

The creature's eyes were entirely black – no white of the eye – and in them she saw herself reflected, tiny and terrified.

Light was coming from her head . . . it was how she could see at all.

Her dream?

A gasp escaped her. Again, the creature flinched.

Her fingers gripped the sheet beneath and she edged away. She saw its human shape. But it was not of this Earth – there were layers of shadowy muscles and sinews as if it was missing a skin, like medical drawings she had seen in books of skinned dead people.

"Oh God . . ."

The creature watched her lips move. It stood upright.

She backed further away, pulling herself up against the headboard and yanking the bedcover around her neck.

Its eyes focused just above hers, boring into her forehead. The light was growing stronger by the second – like the spinning bright halo she'd seen with the messenger.

Its tongue ran over its lips, entranced by her dream.

She knew it wanted to take it from her.

The creature cocked its head as it stared at the bright colours. It tensed and lunged towards her, arm outstretched, extending a barbed black claw – but she dodged. Her halo pulsed even brighter and the creature recoiled, lifting a hand to shield its eyes.

"Better . . ." It spoke. The cracked, strained voice made her skin crawl. "To sleep dreamless is better . . ."

The claw reached for her forehead.

Ruth tilted her head back, shuffling as far away on her bed as she could. "No, it's mine!"

The hands were still moving towards her.

"'Tis too bright . . ." A fleck of spit escaped the creature's mouth as it spoke, and again the creature's hands gestured towards her dream, lifting a knee onto the mattress.

"No!" Ruth shouted, finding more strength.

The creature leaned forwards and closed one hand into a fist. "But dreams . . . bad . . . filled with hope . . . cruel . . ."

Ruth was slowly registering its meaning. "Cruel?"

"Hope – is – CRUEL!" It spoke the words like a mantra and clenched both its smoky hands into fists. "I steals dreams before they does harm."

"But if you steal my hope I will have no future!"

The creature's eyes moved from side to side, as if considering her words. But then a second pair of eyes appeared in the darkness of her room – was she seeing double? Her terror multiplied. A burning smell filled her nose – what was happening? This one was more than a creature of shadows. It smoked with rippling black flames, and in its fist was a bundle of blackened halos. Bile rose in her throat.

"What's going on 'ere?" The dream stealer snarled, and ducked beneath the canopy above her bed, hunching up beneath it to look at Ruth, wide awake. It narrowed its eyes, bared its teeth. "She sees us."

"And her dream . . . so strong!" The first thief was eyeing her dream like a prize.

"Pah!" The dream stealer rippled the sinewy shadows of its body as it pulled its head back and stood upright. "Just get on with it. Yer always makes it a weird kind of ritual, like yer afraid of 'em."

"But dreams . . ."

"Yer soft. Sort her and get a move on – ye drag that stupid sack like yer dragging the world."

It was only then that Ruth noticed the sack the first creature carried. Was it full of dreams?

"But she sees us – hears us!"

"Do it!" The tall creature stalked out through the closed door. Ruth was sick with fear.

The dream stealer would not take its eyes off her dream. And while it continued to stare, Ruth saw one, two, three tiny shadows swirl around the dream thief's formless body, like black snowflakes. More and more shadows appeared, whirled and tumbled. Was this the black snowstorm of her dream?

Then something even stranger took place. Ruth's eyes opened wider still. Over the creature's body appeared a ghostly impression of the same freezing boy she had been dreaming about. It was as though she was seeing double: the boy from her dream and the thief. They were oblivious to each other, yet their movements were almost the same. Even their expressions! The boy looked afraid. And was that fear in the creature's eyes, too? But why would *it* be afraid of *her*?

It reached out a hand towards her dream as the boy reached out his hand as if for help – then dropped it to his side. The boy shadowed its every move.

Her eyes went back and forth between her secret panel and the dream thief. Trembling, she inched along to the edge of her bed and, slowly, put one foot on the floor, then the other. She grabbed her cape from the chair and wrapped it around herself, not once taking her eyes off him.

"You sees me!" He said the words quietly, fear growing in his eyes.

Her breaths were quick. She nodded.

This thief's eyes widened.

Somehow, watching the ghostly boy from her dream reaching out for help, she felt strangely moved.

"Yes, I do. I see you."

He moved around the foot of her bed towards her.

She backed up against the wall, her fingers reaching for the secret panel behind the chair, but unable to find its edge. Words were her only defence, and they spilled out of her.

"My hopes and dreams are everything to me! Without them, I'll have nothing! I would have no strength to carry on! But I will not give up on hope! You cannot do this to me. I will not let you! I would be nothing, my life will be ruined!" Silas came into her mind. Meg too. And the Countess. She had already lost too much.

"But dreams make pain . . ."

The swarming black snow and the ghost-like boy were even closer to Ruth now.

Under her hand she felt the wood give a fraction – the secret panel. She could escape. Yet she hesitated.

"I think I dream about you." Ruth said to the creature. She pointed at her own halo. "This here! I think it's making me dream about you!"

At that revelation, his brow furrowed in a frown.

"Yes, a dream comes to me," she gabbled breathlessly. "Night and day it comes to me, there's black snow and a freezing boy – I see it now, too."

He frowned more deeply, as though trying to make sense of her words. But then something else caught his attention: her little pocket globe on the table. He grabbed it, cupped it in his smoky hand and rolled it in his palm, lifted it up level with his eyes, examining it from every angle.

"I met a messenger who gives dreams to people." Ruth kept her voice low, forcing him to listen to her. "His name is Godrick. He told me to hold fast to my dreams, whatever happens. I cannot, will not, give up, no matter how I feel. I will find a way through, but only if I have my hopes and dreams."

The creature dangled her little globe by its golden chain and pushed it around with a finger to make it rotate. He shook his head as if in disbelief. He was so bewitched he seemed to have forgotten her.

"This thing," the creature murmured.

Ruth watched the boy and the creature holding her little globe.

"I do not know what you are now," she ventured, "but were you once a boy?"

He looked up from the globe, frowning. The ice boy reached out to her again.

She repeated the question. "Were you a boy before . . . before you were like this?"

The creature did not answer but backed away, picked up the sack and clasped Ruth's pocket globe in the other hand. Little by little, he melted into the door, his sack, his shadowy legs, torso, arms. His eyes were the last to go, lingering on her.

"I saw you," Ruth said, lifting her chin, as he completely disappeared.

For a moment she stared, transfixed, after him.

The dream thief had spared her dream and stolen the object that had made her feel the closest to her mother and father, to everything that felt good and true. But it was either that or her dream.

Her mind thundered. She leant against the bed and gripped the bedpost.

Only now did she realise that the glowing embers of the fire in her grate had stopped crackling and were flickering back into life. The deadly silence was broken by the slow tick-tock of the clock outside her door – slower than normal, as though its pendulum was held back. It sped up, reaching its normal pace within ten beats. She had seen beyond the mortal world, and something had happened to time itself. But how could she even see beyond like this – had she suddenly developed second sight? *The London Chronicles* had reported a woman hung for seeing devils. That devilish darkness she had felt the previous night. To see such things was a curse.

She couldn't stay here. Surely those evil creatures would return for her dream!

Her hands shaking, Ruth lit another candle from the fireplace, pushed aside the secret panel, ran down the steps in her bare feet and turned the handle of the door. It was stuck. She shoved it, rattled it and still it did not budge. The Steward must have locked it. The garden was inches away, outside. But she was trapped.

She retreated back up the steps and slowly peeked out from behind the panel into her room. It was empty. She tried the door to the corridor. It opened. The light from her candle trembled over the walls and floorboards. Crowbury Hall was quiet, save for the tick of the clock, in time with her own breaths. She forced herself to concentrate. As long as the flame of her candle kept moving, and the clock kept ticking, she might be safe.

At first she stepped with care, her naked feet bathed in a pool of candlelight that did not stretch far enough. Then she rushed to the windows furthest from the family's empty bedchambers, pressing herself against the walls as she edged along towards the stairs. The candle flame flickered and dimmed – but was this the breeze from the windows or the presence of dream thieves?

"Come on, keep going . . ." she whispered to the candle, as to herself.

Ahead in the darkness, a floorboard creaked. She strained to see, lifting her candle further forwards.

Nothing.

As she turned the corner to the stairs, the candle flame froze.

Her dream was visible once more – shining so brightly! She was rigid with fear.

From the top of the stairs, another creature walked up to her, bold as brass, face to face. It crept around her, lifted a lock of her hair, sniffed it. It drew closer and licked her cheek, ran a probing finger over her lips and down her neck to the hollow above her chest, as though fascinated by her flesh.

Breathing and screaming were both impossible. The palms of her hands were damp. She felt a tear form, brim, and spill over, running down her cheek.

Then the candle slipped out of her sweaty hand.

Seeing her move, the creature made a grab for her dream halo but was thrown down the stairs, as though the dream itself had pushed the thief away.

The only way down to the library was past the fallen creature. Not knowing how many more were behind her, she had no choice. She dashed down the steps, feeling a clawing at her ankle.

21

The Candle

Ruth jumped past the dream thief, ran down the stairs, along the corridor and into the library, closing the door quietly. The room was cloaked in darkness. Even the fusty smell alarmed her. Nowhere was safe. She gripped the handle so tight it would not move, and leant back against the panelling, her weight keeping the door firmly shut. At any moment, a dream thief could pass behind her, stalking her. A hand, a blackened nail, could touch the handle on the other side. She let go, repelled by the thought. Then the memory of that dream thief melting through her door made take a step away. No wall or door could ever protect her from these creatures.

Ruth felt her way to the large table and rifled through the drawer, feeling for a loose candle. She felt a waxy cylinder, pulled it out and shuffled with hands outstretched to the fireplace. She poked the candle around the ashes, finding the fire's dying embers, and a little flame sprang up. She sat back on her heels and let out a breath as the candle threw soft light around the room. Standing to press it into a candlestick, her sudden reflection in the window caught her eye – flickering on the diamond-shaped panes of glass – fractured, as though she had been broken into a hundred pieces. She looked so afraid. So alone.

"Father!" The lips of many Ruths said the word, the image replicated.

Ruth was not sure if she had actually made a sound. Her throat was so tight she could barely swallow.

Gathering all the candles she could lay her hands on, she lit each one and carried the last with her to the chair near the fireplace. Now, candles blazed all around, a sea of little stems of light . . . plenty, but they would not last the night. She blew a few out to save for later.

She drew up her feet into her nightgown and, with the back of her hand, rubbed the dampness from her cheek where the creature had licked her. Revolted, she wiped her hand on the arm of the chair.

Had she become a witch?

How else could she see these creatures, unless she had second sight?

Was heresy close to sorcery? Right here, in this spot, she had listened to those friends of her father's, Dee and Digges. They had talked about proving an unorthodox cosmology that was sacrilegious to men in power. She had revelled in the danger, poured over their heretical book. Her father had hidden it behind her secret panel. That book, kept so close to where she slept . . . perhaps it had infected her mind? These men had opened the heavens to her – but what if they were deceived? Had they exposed her to dark dangers beyond her imagining? If their work was damned, in believing them, had she unleashed devils from hell?

And what of the freezing boy from her dream?

The messenger Godrick was from beyond the mortal world . . . yet he felt like nothing but pure goodness. Surely no sorcery could account for that!

She looked into the candle flame beside her. It rose out of the stem of tallow, the yellow edge touching the air.

"Non Sine Sole Iris," she whispered. The flame wavered and trembled with her breath.

There must be light in this darkness.

Or was this all a nightmare?

If this *was* a dream, the darkest of dreams, she would feel no pain.

She whisked one finger through the flame. The little tongue licked her flesh; too fast to feel anything.

This time, she made herself go slowly and forced her finger to stay in the heart of the flame. Searing pain. She plunged her finger into her mouth.

It was burnt. She was awake. This was real.

If her father was here she could have gone to him, though heaven only knows what he would do. His private writing desk was just to her right with its angled leather top and series of drawers. Leaning over, she pulled one open and fished around to find one of his papers. All she wanted to see was his handwriting to make him feel closer. She found a list, written in his angular style, the paper creased where his hand had rested on it. It noted items to take on a journey: fur cloaks, books, a Theodelitus and other astronomical measuring devices.

Her old comfort, the little globe, now that was gone too . . . if only she had returned it to its place of safety! She glanced at the Cabinet of Curiosities. But something new inside it caught her attention, gleaming in the candlelight. She wiped her eyes and pulled herself upright. No mistake.

A new object lay on the top shelf.

Ruth climbed out of the chair and crept over towards the cabinet. Closer now, she could see it was an old book, a modest size, bound with worn leather straps wrapped tight around it and sealed with red wax, leather smooth as soapstone. How could she not have seen it before?

She fetched the cabinet key from her father's desk, rushed back and unlocked the doors. As she grasped the book, her hand froze. To her right, shadow slid upon shadow.

A dream thief, crouching low, was watching her.

22

Awakening

The dream thief was resting its hand on the crystal Moon inside the Armillary Sphere. It withdrew its arm like a shot, stealing a look at the planets within.

Ruth was rooted to the spot. It was barely visible in the sea of light, a dark void against the familiar items in the library.

The dream thief leaned its head against the brass curves of the Armillary Sphere, rested its hand there, and fixed her with a stare. Their eyes locked together.

Ruth could barely breathe. She had been a fool! With so many candles burning and being so lost in thought, she had not seen her dream halo begin to glow, nor the flames of the fire stilling.

Beside the creature lay a sack on the floor – and her little globe.

Her dream stormed across her vision. The freezing boy sprung to life before the dream thief – a ghost before a shadow, but clear enough that the boy's hazel eyes caught the candle-light. The dark threads around his irises threatened to blacken his eyes.

"Help me," the boy whimpers.

Still crouching together, the double image of the dream thief and the boy came together, merging as one. The thief-boy picked up her family's little globe, gesturing with it as it rocked wildly from side to side. Thinking of her mother's hand holding the chain, anger flashed through her.

"See . . . how did you 'av this?" The thief-boy spoke as one, twitching the chain again.

Ruth breathed in deeply. "It is mine."

The thief-boy stood up, head cocked to one side, staring at her – entranced now with Ruth as much as he had been with the globe.

"'Tis not . . . I knows not . . ."

"Who *were* you?" She was not sure if she was asking the dream thief or the ghostly boy.

"This place . . . all the candles . . ."

The thief-boy looked around, as if seeing the candles for the first time. His gaze returned to Ruth and settled on her forehead. The thief-boy reached out a shadowy hand towards her dream – or was he reaching out for her? He took one step closer, then another. Ruth reached up and put her hands over her dream halo. He hesitated, and shook his head as if in confusion.

"And whose dreams are in there?" Ruth pointed at the sack. She thought of Little Luce. Of Silas. Her heart tightened.

"Those?" He glanced backwards and shrugged. "I know not . . . those is dead."

"Dead dreams?"

"I help . . ."

Her jaw clenched. Little Luce, standing so still . . .

"What you do is the opposite of help! It's evil!"

The thief-boy frowned and retreated, still holding her pocket globe.

"Truly yours?" He twitched the chain and backed away towards the door.

Ruth nodded. "Yes. It was my Grandfather Richard's."

He released the chain as if it was scalding hot. It fell to the rug with a soft thud. The thief-boy stared at it lying there, then up at Ruth, eyes wide.

Next, the thief-boy picked up the sack and glanced around at the stacks and rows of books on dozens of shelves as though daunted by the sight. The merged dream thief and ghostly boy backed away, turning and making for the door.

"Wait! Why do you want to know?" Ruth cried out, but it was too late.

She dashed over to rescue her little globe and, clutching the book from the cabinet, retreated to the chair. She could not stop thinking about the creature's hands touching the globe, and the boy, who had walked straight out of her dream.

There was a blanket draped over the back of the chair, and she pulled it around her, but still her body shook.

Back and forth she looked between the walls and the window, waiting for darkness to lift, willing daylight to come, desperate for this night to be over.

Sleep came close, heavy with intent. By squeezing the globe's sharp catch hard into her palm, she kept herself awake, watching the candles wane.

Outside the window, the writhing black fog dissipated and drifted apart. It was as though a storm had gone . . . as though the creatures had left the hall. But not a muscle in her body could relax – not till the hours of darkness had passed.

With a jolt she realised she had lost track of the candles burning down to their base. Had she drifted in and out of sleep without knowing it? The terror remained that a dream thief could come and steal her dream when she could not protect herself.

She found herself fingering the red wax seal of Crosskeys on the leather binding around the book, and inspected it more closely. Only now did she notice that, unusually, no words were imprinted on the cover to indicate its contents. Were its pages empty too? The seal and bind implied otherwise. And why was it in the cabinet, not on the bookshelves? Who had placed it there when her father was away? He alone curated the Collection of Curiosities, for he alone ventured far enough away to find new things.

To break the seal seemed wrong, but she wanted to see inside. Gently, she cracked the wax, fractured and separated the Crosskeys, and slowly loosened the leather binds wrapped around the book, her fingertip nudging between two pages towards the front. What she glimpsed inside surprised her, for she saw tiny drawings of people. Not daring to open the book fully yet, she flicked the edges of the pages and saw numerous more detailed sketches, each accompanied by notations. To look closer, she opened the book fully. Dust exploded out of its pages. She sneezed and dropped the book, pinching her nose to stop herself from sneezing further, but she sneezed again – so much so it made her eyes water. How could one book contain so much dust!

But then the particles gathered together, an ashy cloud. It hung as if suspended in the air . . . and it moved, eerily, as though it were alive.

The cloud was coughing and spluttering!

Ruth ran behind the chair and hid. The coughing continued. She dared to peek, her eyes widening at what she saw.

23

The Dreams of the Dead

Ruth's fingers gripped the chair. The cloud thickened, solidified and, bit by bit, began to take the form of a man . . . a hip-length cape became clear, an old-fashioned square lace collar at the neck, a waistcoat tightly drawn with cords, striped breeches, green tights, black shoes with clunky metal buckles. He stood as tall as her father, busy batting away the dust from his clothes. As soon as his wide-brimmed black hat had inked in, he swept it off his head and used it to rid himself of the remaining specks of dust. Amidst this cleansing, he glanced over towards the chair behind which she was hiding, his eyes twinkling. He was from a world beyond flesh, yet he looked as real as anyone she knew. In fact, he looked exactly like the man on the road outside her father's warehouse, the one who calmed and steadied her horse.

"Infernal filth . . . from dust we come . . ."

The man spoke to himself as he shook his hat vigorously, ridding it of the last grey flecks. He sneezed violently, rubbed his finger along the bottom of his nose, composed himself, then replaced his hat on his head and glanced around the library.

"Good eve!"

He spoke warmly, as though looking for an old friend.

Ruth did not move and stayed hidden.

He sneezed and spoke again as he picked up the book she had dropped on the floor and placed it on the table beside him, careful to keep the pages spread wide.

"Good eve? There must be another soul present, for a book cannot open itself . . ."

Ruth was staying quiet. After those dream thieves, she could trust nothing. Seeing this now must mean she was going mad!

"The Guardian of Dreams never makes a mistake, and I have been clearly despatched to some place new."

At the mention of the Guardian's name, she felt the same as she experienced with Godrick . . . profound peace like a pebble dropping into deep water inside her. Another Latin phrase came to her, from something she had once read, rising up from the hidden recesses of her memory. *Ut lateat virtus proximate mali. In the midst of evil, good lies hidden.*

Shakily, she stood up.

"Why, gentle lady, we meet again!"

So recognition did not belong to her alone.

She nodded, unsure of what to make of him. Like Godrick, he was not an earthly being, but he too seemed harmless. And if he *was* the helpful man beside her father's warehouse who'd saved her horse . . .

"My name is Adam Blackwood, your good servant from the Guardian of Dreams, here to do your bidding."

The extravagance of his gestures reminded her of an actor who opens a play, addressing the audience with a prologue. What would he go on to say? His eyebrows were so animated they had a life of their own, and his beard and moustache twitched as he spoke. He appeared so entertaining that despite everything, an involuntary smile crept onto her mouth.

"Good eve," replied Ruth at last. "Were you not there . . . earlier . . . on the road?"

Adam grinned at her. "There, indeed, I was. There and here, here and there. I appear in many places for I am the Chronicler of Chronicles."

"Oh! Which chronicles?"

He lifted one finger, twirled it dramatically and pointed down at the book out of which he had appeared.

"This, *The Chronicle of Dreams*." He patted the open pages. "Though I do concede this is not the only one, for there are voluminous volumes. In fact, in their entirety, they contain the dreams of all those who have passed on." He took a breath and fixed her with a stare. "That is to say, the dreams of the dead."

The dreams of the dead! She moved around the chair and sat down, pulling the blanket around her again and bunching up her legs, watching this bizarre figure of a man.

"My role is to assort one particular time that was stupendously spectacular – though I am a little biased," he said, a mischievous twinkle in his eye.

On and on he talked, but Ruth could barely focus on his words because of the questions that jostled in her mind. She was so desperate to make sense of the dream thieves and her dream. Surely, coming from the Guardian of Dreams, he could help her understand.

Ruth shifted in her chair as he waxed on about Columbus, Magellan and Leonardo da Vinci as the greatest examples of dream fulfilment. Never before had she considered that these great men were inspired by their dreams, though this made perfect sense. Everything Adam said was illustrating the things Godrick had said the night before.

"Carried along by their hopes and dreams, they wished to pursue a path of their own in thought and deed, no longer dictated to by those in authority. This great yearning was a fertile pasture for fantastic dreams that inspired inventions and discoveries. Souls would not rest until they pursued the thoughts that burned hot within – and when they did, they felt a soft summer breeze flow through their soul." Adam swayed with the melodrama of his own words.

"Yet dreams are not always sent for a great purpose. Sometimes they are given to suffuse the soul with hope. For without hope, life on Earth is a hideous interlude before heaven."

"Yes!" Ruth cried out, leaning forwards.

Adam nodded and continued.

"Those in power dreaded that these dreaming folk would rise up against them, for their own dreams had been stolen and corrupted by the dream thieves . . . those heaven-hated tyrants!" Adam spat on the floor with violent disgust.

He knew about the dream thieves! A prickle of shock ran over her body.

"Oh I . . ."

Adam did not notice that she had started to speak and charged on.

"And to keep their authority, people in power abused that power. Ignoble nobility, religious men without love, unjust men of justice, kings and queens who vanquished their subjects . . . they abused their power and worked with the dream thieves – those blood-sucking ruinous cankers!" He spat again, as if the words themselves were rotten pieces of fruit.

Working *with* the dream thieves! Ruth wrapped her arms tighter around her legs, feeling suddenly colder. And was this what had happened to Ruth's stepmother? Is this why she was so cruel?

"The authorities crushed any dreaming soul they thought endangered their security. They put a dreadful end to anyone with the temerity to stand foursquare against them, while the dream thieves – those vile loggerheaded pumpions – extinguished hope in the hearts of all those whose dreams they stole, old and young alike. Which brings me to the point of my appearance."

Adam fiddled with his pocket and pulled out a small object, concealing it in his hand.

"Gentle lady," Adam inclined his head. "The Guardian wishes you to receive this."

He stepped forwards and held out to her his closed fist. With a theatrical flourish, he revealed a small vial: a tiny ornate glass bottle with a stopper in the neck. He handed it to Ruth, with a warning not to drop it. She took it in both hands, surprised at its weight when it looked as light as a feather. He told her that it contained something very precious: the tears of children whose dreams had been stolen.

She looked at him. How could such a thing even be possible?

Adam's eyes were alight, full of feeling. With a slight shake in her hand, she lifted the vial to the candlelight, bewitched by the dewy contents. It ought not to look beautiful, but it did. Hundreds of tears made up this liquid, each a moment of sadness or fear captured mysteriously by the Guardian of Dreams. Children through time, whose tears were counted as precious. Her mind turned to those who might have been robbed of their dreams at night, like Little Luce. She remembered seeing her friend standing motionless, her face downcast, and imagined a tear splashing to the ground. Now she wished with all her heart that she had gone to comfort her, and bitterly regretted it.

"The Guardian of Dreams said that you, gentle lady, are young in years and yet you are a true gentlewoman with a noble heart. Already you carry the tears of others in your soul, and you will carry this vial well."

This little glass vial was even more precious than her pocket globe. It was the most precious thing in the world. Perhaps it was a sign that the Guardian knew of her tears, too, and understood what was at risk. She recalled the vision showing her how a dream was made. Or perhaps it was a blessing, something that would give her the strength she needed to hold on to her hopes and dreams. She shivered. She was being given something much more than this vial.

"I . . . little has been making sense," she said. "I have been suffering terrible dreams . . . and when I saw a messenger last night, my soul lifted . . ."

Adam's eyebrows rose, and he nodded eagerly.

"Though I feared I was under some kind of enchantment," she continued. "But tonight when I saw the dream thieves–"

"*You've* seen them?!"

Adam flopped down in the chair opposite her, and for the first time since he arrived, he seemed to stop performing. "Those ravenous wolves!" He spat on the floor, just missing the rug. "*I* cannot see them! None of us can, not us, not the messengers, nor the Guardian. They are a diabolical mystery, for they are made of profound darkness."

"Yes, I see them!"

"Oh, poor child." Adam thoughtfully stroked his moustache, then eyed her – was he wary of her for seeing them? It touched an even deeper fear in her.

"Here – this night, for the first time! One in this room," Ruth gestured over towards the Armillary Sphere, "but it has gone!"

Adam, astonished, looked around him.

"Have I become a witch?" Ruth asked quickly.

Adam shook his head. "Why should you think that?"

"How else could I see the dream thieves? I have exposed myself to heresy . . . I even enjoyed it."

"But that is not the same as sorcery. What heresy?"

"One that exalts the Sun above the Earth, placing it at the centre of the heavens, making Earth the smaller of the two."

"But that is correct." Adam spoke with a small smile on his face. He tapped his fingers on the arm of the chair and looked at her with a gleam in his eye.

"*What* did you say?" Ruth was agog. For now, this quietened all the other questions in her mind.

"The Sun, gentle lady, *is* at the centre of the heavens. That is the true order of things, and this fact is in the process of becoming known in these years. Truth presses through dreams at the right time, so 'tis inevitable that certain things are explored. This pattern of people dreaming up similar questions and ideas at similar times happens all the way down through the years. To question is never wrong; the Guardian loves a questioner. Truth rises up through hopes and dreams."

Ruth struggled to take it in. "'Tis true? And another dream will inspire another person to prove it – and even the authorities will come to accept it?"

"Yes. It will be mathematically proven in a matter of years. It is not heresy, gentle lady. One day it will be unthinkable that people believed otherwise, like the Earth being round, not flat. This 'heresy' is not the reason you have seen dream thieves, rest assured. It will be for some other reason that you've been able to see them."

Ruth let out a long, slow breath.

"Gentle lady, the Guardian of Dreams *wants* people to question the existing state of affairs. Dreams from the Guardian, whether they feel foul or fair, impart intuitions and ideas and hopes that spur you into good action. Your dream still spins. You, for one, survived your encounter with the dream thieves – this time, at any rate. Let us pray you never see one ever again."

Ruth thought of her dreams of black snow. She held up the vial of tears to the candlelight, and spoke slowly, not taking her eyes off the bottle.

"Adam, could you show me the dream of one whose tears may be held in here – whose dream was stolen?"

"A most unusual request, young lady!"

"But can you? Might . . . this person be in your Chronicle of Dreams?"

"It is possible. They contain those whose dreams were stolen, as well as those for whom their dreams became the uniting feature of their lives, so it is, in fact, a request that, well . . ." Adam jumped up from the chair and bowed low before her. "I can indeed help you. Information is my name. Information is my nature. What was the name?"

Ruth shook her head. "I know not."

Adam frowned. "Zounds. Do you have a portrait, so I might at least recognise him?"

Ruth pictured the freezing boy from her dream. "If I saw him, I might recognise him. I believe he came here to Crowbury Hall."

She stood up, put the vial of tears into the pocket of her nightgown, and walked to the Armillary Sphere, its solid brass glowing in the candlelight. She tapped a finger on it. "He is in some way connected to this and . . ." She stopped speaking mid-sentence.

Adam span around on his heel in a circle, and slapped his forehead with his hand.

"I'm a chronicler, not a wizard! But what, gentle lady? Why have you sat down on the floor?"

Ruth pressed her hands into the rug beneath her knees, and held her breath. The Armillary Sphere and all its magnificent globes to her right, set in their deadly wrong places. The Curiosity had been presented to King Henry, the night of the feast that her grandfather had written about, and the boy, Master Curiosity, had spoken heresies. She, of all people, could understand this.

"What has befallen you?"

Still Ruth would not reply, her face cast downwards.

"Gentle lady?"

Ruth breathed deeply and looked up at Adam though her hair.

"Master Curiosity. I think that was his name – or at least the name he was known by."

"So we do have a name," mumbled Adam as he immediately took *The Chronicles* and, keeping the end papers far apart, leafed expertly through the rest of the pages, as though flicking through a pack of cards.

"Master Curiosity . . . he knew my grandfather . . . and he would have met his sister Mary, and their father, too. He knew my family . . . and he will have met King Henry."

For a few moments, Ruth did not move. If she was correct, it was no wonder that her dream had so disturbed the creature's darkness. Many threads connected the two of them. Was this why she could see him – and therefore the other dream thieves too? But Adam was looking through his *Chronicles*, trawling through the dreams of the dead, and she did not want to miss this.

She moved closer, peering at the flicking pages, entranced. It was as though the book had sprung into life. Each minute figure stood upright as it was revealed for a brief moment on the page, a miniature of the real person, topped by a tiny dream halo. As Adam slowed his pace, Ruth saw that some of the figures were babies, others children, others older. Why were they all different ages, she wondered. Perhaps it represented when each person had died? She bit her lip. Her own mother . . . would she be in here? Of what had she dreamt – and what of her hopes and dreams for her daughter?

But, greater than this was Ruth's craving to see the boy from her dreams. She looked even closer. Adam paused and lifted one finger.

"Don't ever let the pages close fully, young lady, or I shall disappear with them, for this is the way I travelled here. The Chronicles must be kept open."

Ruth shrugged, thinking about the boy from her dream – when he wasn't playing Master Curiosity, wasn't he Jude, the young candle-maker? The son of the vicious man Grandfather Richard had written about? That was why the ghostly boy had noticed the candles. No wonder the black snow had blown across her sight two days ago in town, as she had passed by the old candle-maker's shop.

"Hmmm." Dissatisfied, Adam turned to the back of *The Chronicles*, slid his thumb between two pages and opened the book right in the middle. He pulled a magnifying glass from his pocket and peered.

"Aha!" he said triumphantly, offering the glass to Ruth.

She looked through the lens. There were more figures, now crystal-clear. Young men in clothes from different countries . . . princes . . . soldiers . . . sportsmen . . . none appealed to her. She turned the page. There were knights dressed in gleaming armour and battle-soiled chainmail. These left her cold too, as did the religious men, both the haughty and the humble. She flipped over several more pages, coming to every rank of servant.

One thin young lad caught her eye, dressed in ragged breeches and a tunic, with greasy hair and a proud, jutting chin.

Ruth watched his dream pulse with rainbow colours before darkening. Black shadows dissembled and whirled around his body just like the black snow. Ruth stared and shivered. It *was* him! The ice boy from her dream, the victim of another dream thief in another time. His hopes and dreams had been so twisted and perverted that, in stealing other people's dreams, he believed he was right in dream-stealing. Staring at Master Curiosity's tiny dream, she remembered the halo around her own head and that vision Godrick had shown her.

Ruth twisted her hair into a knot. She looked up at Adam, a question in her mind. When she could see into her own dream when awake, could she not also see into someone else's?

24

Shadows Beyond Time

"Can you take the dream out of The Chronicles?"

Ruth pointed at the tiny ragged boy on the book.

The Chronicler paced around the library. Ruth asked again.

"Gentle lady, this is most irregular!" He scratched his head through his hat, then thought better of it, took it off and scratched his head again. "It is a rare enough event that The Chronicles are presented to anyone outside of –"

"Please," Ruth pressed, feeling a hot quickening. "It's important."

"I can tell you information about the dream and that should suffice."

"But can you tell me about his life?"

He let out a sigh. "No."

"And if you helped me to watch his dream, I might find out more?"

Adam scratched his head again. "Well, yes."

"So?"

Adam frowned. "I must warn you. Such an undertaking can have a profound effect on a mortal."

Ruth paused. An idea was growing, a possible way to intervene, but to make it work she needed to find out as much as she could about Jude. The Chronicler would never approve of her plan – he had already said he never wanted her to meet another dream thief.

"You see, 'tis the only way I can understand the boy's feelings."

"His feelings?! You hardly knew his name!"

"I cannot explain why, but I need to find out." She returned to the Armillary Sphere and touched the vast brass spheres.

"Well. If you insist, but again I must warn you that his dream was stolen – see, 'tis black there, at the end." He pointed at the little dream, but seeing she would not give in, shook his head in resignation. "As you will," he said crisply. "Sit down here." He motioned at a chair.

He extracted tiny circular pincers from the breast pocket of his waistcoat, fixed them around the edge of the minute halo, pulled a lever then extracted it from *The Chronicles*. He set it firmly on Ruth's head, as though locking it into place, which seemed almost silly as it was so small. She felt a tremor inside. She gripped the arms of the chair.

He stood back and watched, hands on hips. She kept her eyes on him, feeling strange, and saw his mouth purse with concentration as he stared at the dream halo.

Within a few moments, the halo was spinning and swelling in size until it was flowing around her forehead before her eyes. Her vision was flooded with lilac, blue, green, yellow, red. The rainbow colours danced faster and faster, blurring into white. Adam's candlelit face and the shelves of books faded from her sight as the dream subsumed her.

Ruth sees a hand – not her own, but the boy's – holding a feather quill, roughly drawing a diagram of globes with arcs made of dotted lines, perhaps showing their trajectory across the sky. It's the last thing she would have expected of the bedraggled-looking lad. The sheen of wet ink dulls as the rough vellum paper absorbs each line. The fingers of his left hand are tensed, keeping open the pages of another book. He is copying what he sees. Candlelight flickers over his desk: the rest of the room is in darkness. Jude closes the papers and places a cover page on top: *On the Revolution of the Heavenly Orbs*. Copernicus's banned book – Jude could be making the amateur copy that was kept secretly behind her bed! Her heart races as she feels the boy's elation and concentration – seeing into his dream could change everything.

He looks upwards as moonlight suddenly shines down – and there, through a skylight, is the twinkling night: the subject of so much consternation. The moon is almost full. Soft light cascades down and illuminates the sparse, dusty room.

Jude glances down and touches his bruises – his shins and arms are covered with them. Ruth feels his distress and recalls what Grandfather Richard wrote about the candle-maker . . . if the fists were his father's, they would pummel his heart too.

The boy is clearing his throat. "Your Majesty." He gets up and gesticulates as he walks around, as though rehearsing a speech, checking now and again what he is saying against notes neatly piled to one side of his desk. Ruth understands that he is rehearsing a Master Curiosity speech.

Everything blurs, as though time is speeding forwards, and the vision comes to rest on a riot of lords and ladies. They surround Jude, busily conversing and feasting on huge platters of food. Through his eyes, she recognises the distinctive wooden panelling and fireplace – it is her own banqueting chamber. She feels Jude's great happiness as the crowd applaud him, and from the boy's tremendous peace, she wonders if it is approval that Jude dreams of. It would make sense, given his father's beatings; the boy would be desperate for approval from other people.

Now a man towers over Jude with fearsome eyes – one who wears the Royal chain, one who can only be a King. She recognises the face, and the ginger and grey-flecked hair and beard from paintings, and knows that Jude was presented to Henry the Eighth, Queen Elizabeth's father. So this must be him. Everyone falls silent as the King speaks, but his words are distorted as though the dream is faltering. Is this where it starts to blacken?

"Yes, curious indeed, Master Curiosity, an entertaining notion."

His words are drenched in sarcasm, when they could have meant the opposite, and as he speaks the colour drains out of the dream. Now everything is in shades of black, and shadows swarm around Jude like the black snow. They obscure the King's face as he spits out cruel words and casts Jude's notes onto a roaring fire, the shadows mingling with black ash drifting up the chimney. Beyond, the crowd is completely altered – they jeer and laugh.

A cold hand closes around his heart and she feels this as vividly as if it were her own. Icy fingers push into his veins, but she determines to bear it for as long as possible so she can understand how he becomes a dream thief.

The boy runs. He stumbles his way through the town until he reaches the monastery. The place is in ruins. Stones, timber, glass scattered everywhere – so different to how it looked to her the day before.

He kneels on wet cold stone, cradles himself as if for comfort or in protection, and rocks back and forth, all the while muttering words like a chant.

"Better a stone heart than a heart that hurts . . .

Better stone ears than ears that hear . . .

Better a stone soul than a soul that hopes . . .

Stone heart . . . stone ears . . . stone soul . . ."

Ruth feels a dreadful darkness envelop her body, a hateful poisonous bitterness . . . a desire to destroy hope.

"GET IT OFF ME!" Ruth yelps, her hands clawing at the dream, scratching with her nails to try to remove it.

Adam was there in an instant. He twisted it, pulled once, twice, and plucked the dream from her head. It was black. Immediately, it began to shrink.

"I know not . . . it was terrible." Ruth slumped in the chair, wiped her eyes on her arm and watched warily as Adam returned Jude's dream to *The Chronicles*.

"I saw what happened to him when his dream was stolen! It was like a record of the end of his days, when all went wrong."

"I did forewarn you," Adam said quietly, bending over *The Chronicles* as he fitted the now-tiny dream to the little figure on the page.

Ruth hugged a cushion to her chest and was silent for a while. Adam turned away from the book and sat down in the chair opposite, playing with the ends of his moustache as he studied her.

"I understand more. The others . . . the ones who were cruel to him . . . were their dreams stolen too?" The Countess, the Steward and Silas came to her mind.

Adam nodded. "Yes. Maybe I should have told you and spared you the fear."

She shook her head. "I had to see for myself." It was all she had to say. Minutes passed as she curled up in the chair, rubbing her cold feet, exhausted. "I've read about Jude in my grandfather's journals, Adam. As Master Curiosity, he would come and present the objects to the King – the things inside there," she gestured with her hand towards the cabinet. Then she moved her hand along, pointing to the Armillary Sphere. "But the night he presented *that*, it all went wrong. He disappeared and could not be found. My grandfather searched everywhere. They did not even find his body."

Adam shrugged, looking at her quizzically.

"Is that not peculiar?" She looked at him carefully. She made even more rapid connections.

Adam tapped his fingers on the arm of the chair. "Not all bodies are found."

"Can I assume that your Chronicles only account for dreams – it is not a catalogue of deaths? Of manner of death, I mean?"

"That is fair to say," he admitted, his eyebrows raising in the middle, now curious too.

"Dear sir, is it also fair to say that though . . . though you are very learned, you do not know everything?" Ruth ventured her private thought about this magical man from the Guardian of Dreams, surprised at her own boldness.

"We cannot see everything, that is true, so we cannot know quite everything, though we know a great deal," Adam said, frowning as he waited for her next comment.

Ruth paused.

"Adam, one child disappeared from Crowbury yesterday. It was the blacksmith's son. Perhaps another child disappeared tonight, God forbid." She scowled. "Despair overwhelmed Jude. I felt it. I'm afraid the same will happen to the blacksmith's lad and anyone who's gone tonight! Jude's bitterness was so severe, I believe it turned him into a dream thief."

"A dream thief!" Adam jumped up from the chair and spat noisily. "Those dissembling invisible harpies!"

"Yes! He was the first thief I met this night. I'm sure of it. He was fascinated by my pocket globe and the spheres, as if he had seen them before. You see, he steals hopes and dreams because he believes he is doing the right thing-"

"Stop! STOP!" Adam interrupted, his eyes blazing. He pulled his hat from his head and threw it onto the floor. "No, no, NO! The villainous two-faced hell-born miscreant! You're telling me you spoke to a dream thief and he persuaded you he was human?" He paced back and forth.

"Yes and no . . . not persuaded . . ."

"Yes or No?!" Adam demanded, turning to face her. "The bat-fouling murderous mangy-dog has won your sympathy?"

"Not truly," she said cautiously.

"But he's a dream thief! You cannot trust one word that comes from the mouth of that spleeny death-token!"

"I do not know . . ."

"You cannot help them! Their foul deeds place them a thousand miles from the hope of any redemption," Adam said, gesturing wildly.

"But what if he, or if some of the others, were once human? I saw two others and they felt like damned devils who've never walked this Earth. But this one is different. I believe it is – was – Jude, the candlemaker's boy. He is asking for help. He doubts his thieving. He did not steal my dream and I believe he wants to stop, and perhaps he *could* with–"

Adam slammed his fist on the table. "NO! You interfering clotpole!"

Ruth took a step back, raising one hand in caution, and spoke with even greater conviction. "*You* did not speak to him."

"Do not meddle in things not meant for you! Take care for you are making haste!" Adam wagged his finger at her.

"You said that before to me on the road out of Crowbury, but you were wrong then and you are wrong now. What I had to do could not wait!"

"At the cost of almost breaking your horse's leg. This won't be the half of it if you carry on this path! There's too much at stake!"

Anger grew in Ruth. "You don't know what is being forced upon me, what is being stolen from me!"

Her life was not the only one in jeopardy. The blacksmith's lad, vanished, the butcher's nieces and nephews so quiet, and Little Luce, a shadow of herself . . . not that she knew what was really happening at that point. She could not have made a difference then.

But now she could.

Ruth pressed her lips together. She could not give up. She felt inside her pocket for the vial of children's tears and clasped it with resolve. The Guardian of Dreams knew her deeply enough to generate her dreams – and her dream of black snow had led her to these conclusions – so surely the Guardian *was* inspiring her to do something?

She might not be right, but she had to try. Slowly she took her hand out of her pocket.

Then she lunged for *The Chronicles* and could not stop herself from glancing at Adam. The whites of his eyes showing, he turned, trying to keep the pages open.

But he was too slow. Ruth was quicker, throwing herself over *The Chronicles*, closing it tight and clasping it against her chest.

Adam looked aghast as he saw his body begin to disintegrate. He began to cough as he returned to a cloud of dust, which fell to the carpet.

Ruth was left alone in the silence and darkness of the night, eyes blinking.

25

The Dead of Night

Dream-robbed Crowbury was deathly quiet. In the doorway opposite the old candle-maker's shop, Ruth crouched low. Her eyes hunted the shades of darkness in and around the doorway and rickety windows on the opposite side of the street. Her heart raced from running, carrying the weight of *The Chronicles*. Her breaths came out too fast and too loud, misting the air. To keep her dream halo hidden – should it start to shine – Ruth yanked her hood further forwards. She scrutinised the building for any sign of life, for shadows to slide and move. But there was nothing. Only candles piled high on the sills, crowding the shop. All was still.

She whispered the Guardian of Dreams' name, her breath surging – all the way there she had called on the Guardian, her every step a plea. She was in complete dread of seeing dream thieves. A sea of bedroom windows swam everywhere, above and all around. She scanned for shadowy creatures, but there was no movement there either. Had they left the town? She fiercely hoped so – all but one. His presence at the candle-maker's might tell her that she was right. And it was the only way she could identify him from the others.

The air was filled with the stench of rotting animals – Ruth knew they boiled carcasses to make tallow for the candles. It filled her nostrils. She wrinkled her nose with disgust.

A few sighs, a moan, nearby. Ruth flinched.

It came from an alleyway. A pair of murmuring lovers. They moved on.

The sound of retching made her look around. A door had opened along the street – a drunk man was spilling out of the tavern, wiping his mouth with the back of his hand as he went. The landlord pushed him further out, slammed and locked the door behind him. The man staggered away.

Blinking, she turned her eyes back to the candle-maker's – did that shadow move? The night was so deep it was almost impossible to see any unnatural darkness. No . . . there was nothing.

She steadied herself. She felt so strange, as if the world she knew had collided with another. What was she doing here, risking all? Then the missing young lad came to mind with his flat cap and outsize boots, and Little Luce playing with her long fair hair. She knew exactly why she was here. *Ut lateat virtus proximitate mali.* Good lies hidden, somewhere in this evil . . .

Without looking away from the shop, she felt inside the hunting bag, rooting around *The Chronicles* for the curved shape of the little vial of tears, the gift from the Guardian of Dreams. As she held it between her fingers, it drew her eye downwards. The vial was a tiny miraculous thing, though its glass was dull in this darkness.

She looked up. A shadow shifted. This time she was in no doubt.

Holding her breath, she approached the doorway through the slush and the mud and whispered a name.

But she had been wrong about the shadow. It was nothing.

Ruth's insides turned over. Suddenly, a movement to her right. Out of the butcher's doorway, stepped the faint figure of a dream thief.

In his hand was a sack, dragging on the ground. Ruth spoke his name.

Her dream burst out bright. His face turned towards her.

"W-what did you say . . .?"

Ruth said the name again, gathering all her courage.

"Jude."

She could only just detect the creature's shape as he cocked his head. It was harder to see in these mottled, dirty narrow lanes hemmed in by high buildings. Moonlight struggled to reach down through a break in the storm clouds.

Ruth took an unsteady step, closer. "Good eve, Jude, for I think that is your name."

She hoped that hearing his name, gently spoken, would pierce through his bitterness and reach his heart – if something of his soul did remain. She was sure she'd seen glimmers of it earlier that night . . . that fear in his eyes . . . that fascination with objects once important to him as long-forgotten memories appeared to stir. He returned her gaze with that same look of fascination . . . of curiosity. Master Curiosity. He did not even look for her dream.

"Jude," the dream thief repeated softly. A realisation. A coming back to himself. His hand let go of the sack and he slid down the wall to the ground. It was as though his name was a key, turning and unlocking memories that whirled through him. Grief grew and poured out as a moan, louder and louder.

Ruth saw the ice boy from her dream, the victim of another thief from long ago. His hopes and dreams had been frozen.

"It is you, Jude? The candle-maker's son?"

He looked dazed, but did not deny it.

Trembling, she forced herself to step towards him, pulling the hood of her cape further forwards to conceal her dream. She was so close, she could touch him. And he could touch her.

She had to know for sure.

"Just tell me it *is* you, Jude."

She leant against the doorway, her legs weak, feeling its reassuring solid mass as she focused on the insubstantial shape of the shadowy creature in front of her.

He nodded.

She let out a short sigh, her relief tempered by dread. It was unlikely that Jude was the only human to have undergone this evil transformation.

"'Tis this place . . . so changed . . . I thought I'd forgotten it . . ."

Ruth's father had told her that Crowbury had sprawled in recent years with more dwellings and shops, as well as higher and higher storeys being built on top of the older buildings around the market square. He had told her that, half a century past, the glass windows were just shabby draughty holes with clumsy shutters. Crowbury Hall had grown too, with another storey on top.

He lifted his face towards her. "But that globe . . . here again . . . I knew it . . ." He barely focused on her as he spoke. "That ship . . . there was so many times, so many places . . . backwards and forwards. You would not believe it . . . such things I've seen . . ." The dream thief frowned.

Ruth could barely take in what he said. She felt tears prick her eyes.

"Stealing dreams?"

"Gettin' rid of hope, 'tis too cruel . . ." His words were mechanical, as though all conviction had gone. "So tired . . ."

"Get rid? No," said Ruth firmly.

"I hate hope. It hurt me. And there . . ." Jude pointed to the candle-maker's next door. He winced. Old memories seemed to rise up like blows. He cowered on his knees, hiding his head in his arms, and began to rock. He was falling deeper into the abyss of grief.

Her hand darted out to touch his. Jude looked at her hand as she withdrew it. She glanced down, registering the cold shadows her fingertips had sensed for one moment. It was the strangest sensation.

"I understand how alone you must have felt, how betrayed, but Richard at Crowbury Hall, he tried to help you, did he not?" She suggested the idea so gently. All those times spent pouring over her grandfather's journals – never could she have imagined needing the knowledge for such a time as this. But would her words reach him?

Slowly, Jude raised his head. "R-Richard?"

"He made you Master Curiosity because he saw you were curious about the world –"

"– I weren't curious. Just stupid."

Ruth took a deep breath and crouched down beside the dream thief.

"Richard liked your curiosity, Jude. He wanted to help make your life better. 'Tis true, Jude, is it not? He wanted to help you."

"F-father called him a meddling bastard . . . called me stupid." He lowered his eyes.

"Jude, I read all my grandfather's journals. It is how I realised who you . . . the way you . . . oh I do not know how to say it! But I read his account of that night, at the feast at the Hall when you . . . vanished. Richard never wanted to miss your presentation, but he had no choice."

Jude looked up.

"Yes, it was because of the King, who liked Richard's sister, Mary, so Richard was keeping her away from the banquet that night – you must know what happened to King Henry's wives! He'd killed so many! Can you not see? Everything that happened that night, it was all because of the dream thieves! Everything went sour and twisted because of them! *Everything!*"

"Because of them . . .?"

Ruth nodded. "You and I, Jude, our lives are linked." Even as she said it, she knew she believed it. "I never knew my grandfather but he loved my mother dearly and he cared for you too. My mother read the journals to me, even as a little girl. The journals are still in the library, where you were tonight!"

Jude gazed at her. Ruth could see something was stirring deep within him.

"You recognised the globe and Armillary Sphere from long ago because they had felt part of you. Jude, if nobody's dream had been stolen, none of it would have happened to you. Your father would not have been the way he was. Nor the King. None of it would have happened! And did you know that my grandfather searched for you but could not find you?"

"Oh!" Jude looked up sharply. "He looked for me?" Jude wrapped his arms around his legs and pulled them close. "I didn't know."

"Yes, he looked for you. Jude, you were more important to him than you knew."

She knew from her journals that her grandfather would have intervened, had he been at the feast, and it would not have been a disaster. And she knew from Jude's dream that he had longed for acceptance – if he had not been so humiliated and hurt, time and time again, he would have held onto hope.

After crouching for so long, Ruth's haunches ached and she stood up awkwardly, rubbing her legs, waiting to see what he would do next.

Jude put his head in his hands again. For a moment he hesitated, taking it all in. Then he rocked back and forth on his heels. "I got it so wrong, all wrong. I thought I was doing good! I took the brightest dreams 'cos I wanted to save children 'cos their hopes would turn bad!"

Ruth heard whining sounds. They were coming out of his mouth.

"What 'av I done?" Jude slapped his shadowy head with the heels of his palms.

Ruth reached for his hands to restrain him, but hesitated again, afraid of touching his shadowy body. "I told you, you did not know at the time. You were their victim."

There was only one way to find out whether her revelations had changed him and made him trustworthy, and it would shock him, snap him out of his despair. Ruth braced herself, ready to run away, and inched back her hood to reveal her dream: a perfect, whole, spinning halo. It glowed ever brighter, pulsing dream colours through the darkness, down towards Jude.

Jude stared up in wonder at this girl with dreamlight radiating down over her long, loose hair. He was transfixed . . . this girl, standing fearless before a dream thief . . .

Ruth's dream colours soaked his smoky body as though hope itself was reaching out and touching him. Already tonight her dream had disturbed his darkness, and Ruth uttered a desperate prayer that it would now banish his bitterness.

She watched for a hand coming towards her, a nail extending to score through the whorls of her dreamlight, but he did nothing. His shadows were drenched. She knelt beside him.

At last he spoke. "You're flesh and blood, his flesh and blood – Richard's." Her heart was big and strong, as his had been.

She nodded. In his dark eyes she could see the reflection of her dream and her face beneath it, crowned with dreamlight. His fingers did not flicker . . . the expression in his eyes did not harden . . . surely, then, no part of him wanted to steal it.

He spoke again. "P'raps that's why you could see me?"

Ruth nodded. "Yes, I believe so, yes."

"You're kindly, like him."

Then Jude tore his eyes away from this human girl, suddenly searching the street.

"But the others, Miss, they'll come for your dream! They'll be back for more once the new dreams come."

Ruth blinked. How could she ever dare fall asleep again? It was what she had dreaded in the library. She thought of the messengers, delivering new dreams, and the dream thieves, stealing them.

"They will come again for my dream?" Ruth asked, almost in a whisper.

"They will." He powered to his feet and flexed his shadowy fingers. "And for the new ones that always come to replace the lost ones. Just a question of when. How did you even dodge 'em coming 'ere?"

"I came the back way, through the graveyard."

"Eh?"

"The dead do not dream," Ruth said quietly and stood up, instinctively touching her bag containing *The Chronicles*.

Jude shrugged and spoke quickly. "Us, we never touch the dead. See, I think bitterness stopped my thinkin'. After – after it happened – I went from wantin' to know everythin' to knowin' nothin'. The ship . . ."

Ruth looked away, and back again, registering what he said this time with more force. "Ship?"

Jude glanced skyward. "The ship up there. Can't you see it?"

Gripping the doorway hard, Ruth tilted her head upwards.

At first there was nothing out of the ordinary, only boiling storm clouds, and a break in the coverage where she saw moonlight and stars speckling the night sky beyond. She peered again. Goosebumps broke out over her skin. A black patch was blotting out the stars – a hull, the prow pointing downriver towards London; it was floating high above the Thames.

"Jude, a young boy from the village disappeared last night, and there may be others from Crowbury who have vanished since. Were they taken up there? Is that where they could be?"

Jude nodded.

She hesitated, then expressed the nagging fear she'd felt ever since she had realised Jude's identity.

"Will they become dream thieves?"

"P'raps, if they suffered much."

She covered her mouth to stop herself from gasping out loud. Jude was no exception. Humans *could* be turned into dream thieves!

She recalled her rage at her stepmother and the terrible anguish she felt over Silas and that girl Betsy . . . feelings so powerful they were imprints in her body, and if she had not encountered the dream thieves, if nothing had happened since, no doubt she would still be sobbing and raging on her bed. She had found hope – and so she kept on. But what if she felt no hope at all? What if she were betrayed again and again, if everyone she loved turned against her or abandoned her – Nurse and the falconer and the others? If *all* her hopes and dreams were crushed like a little skull beneath a heel, she imagined it would be easy to be overcome by the despair that Jude had felt: the difference between them was not that great. Yes, if she were to suffer too much, she could imagine hating hopes and dreams. Even she could be turned.

Jude stared at this girl of courage.

Ruth glanced down at her own hands and saw them quivering. She let out a sharp breath. Opening the flap of the hunting bag, she touched the vial of tears and *The Chronicles*, both of which she dared not leave behind. The Guardian of Dreams had sent both to her. And Adam. Godrick, too. Her task was far from over. The dream thieves would come after her, whether she tried to fight them or not.

She puffed out her cheeks and looked at the dream thief before her – and the sack in his hand. The idea that came to her was more frightening than anything she had ever done. But she had to do it. Because if she could help to put things right, she must. She had been right about the dream thief's identity, and she had to trust herself that this idea was not madness, too.

"Jude, perhaps you can help repair some of what has been lost?"

26

Where Thieves Dwell

Up, up and up they climbed, higher and higher above Crowbury, with Ruth inside the sack swung over Jude's shoulder. She felt the bump of every step as he stalked up the long gangplank, ever closer to the dream thieves' ship. Her arms, back and legs ached from curling so tightly. Dread was growing. The shadow of the hull fell over them. Her chest tightened as the criss-cross weave before her eyes grew lighter with her dreamlight. She pulled her hood over the halo as far as it would go, almost covering her eyes, blinking rapidly.

Through a little hole in the sack, she saw Crowbury turn around below . . . the jumble of rooftops . . . the church steeple and graveyard . . . acres of their wood . . . the spiral brick chimneys of Crowbury Hall . . . the river curled as a lock of hair . . . and beyond, miles away, faint moonlit villages turning around as though the Earth had been flicked and sent spiralling through the heavens. All slept while she was carried closer and closer to the dream thieves' ship, as her world – the mortal world – fell away. Sickly dizziness hollowed out her chest as they neared the source of such sorrow and despair.

Soon black fog engulfed the pair of them, obscuring the view. But this was no earthly cloud, for it was broken into little dots . . . it was black snow . . . howling . . . writhing. Coldness crept into her bones the higher they climbed, as if they were descending into a tomb and not climbing into the sky.

Her dream may have led her here . . . but their plan to smuggle her aboard seemed like lunacy. Her head churned. If, God forbid, the dream thieves found her, what would they do? Her hand flexed around the bag containing the Guardian's vial of tears and *The Chronicles*. It was not just herself in danger. In one swoop, the thieves could capture as many dreams as stars in the sky.

In the deepening darkness, dreamlight trickled from beneath her hood and lit up the crosshatch threads of the sack once again. There was nothing she could do to stop it.

A deathly stench filled her nose and seeped into her lungs. She blinked in even greater alarm and peered out through another little hole. The hull was covered in a shimmering black substance: writhing maggots and insects, wriggling under the sheen of blackness smothering the ship. There were moving limbs, like an unborn child skimming the underside of a pregnant belly . . . arms, legs, barely human heads . . . moving as though trapped. She turned her head away. Whatever it was, it reeked of decay.

Black shadows swarmed thicker still and blocked Ruth's vision. But what was this? Deafening moans and wails filled the air and invaded her mind. Her stomach lurched. The intensity of evil diminished her dream; at least it would help her stay hidden. Surely such radiating evil would seep back into Jude's soul? Down in the town he had promised to help. But only an hour ago he had been destroying the future of children everywhere. Were she and Jude allies or enemies? Ruth no longer knew. How could she have even dared to believe that this had been the right thing to do? And what had become of Jude in the past few minutes?

He swung the sack off his shoulder and lifted it high as he stepped onto the deck. She pulled herself even smaller, scared even to breathe. They boarded the ship.

The sound of moaning fog receded, drowned out by the thumping and scraping of mechanical ship sounds. Brisk commands were shouted. Through the hole, Ruth could just make out ropes being flung across the deck, thudding heavily onto greasy planks. Shadowy legs were lining up ahead in some kind of queue. She suppressed a gasp at the sight of so many dream thieves, many of whom were carrying sacks, each one presumably full of dreams. Some hitched the sacks over their shoulders and clutched more halos in their hands. All these dreams . . . from Crowbury and God knew where else. She glimpsed an opening in the timbers ahead, down which they were dropping the dreams, and strained to see more clearly. It must lead below deck. Surely Jude did not plan to throw her down there, after the dreams? This was not what he said he would do.

Other dream thieves, perched on the ship's rail, hooped dead dream halos over their arms and twirled them around their wrists as if they were stolen trinkets, not the hopes and dreams of some poor soul. They leapt onto the deck and cast their plunder down the hole after the others.

The sound of creaking rigging up above caught her attention and she moved her head, finding another hole in the sack she could see out from. There were even more shadowy creatures up there, repairing the sails, running up and down the swinging ropes, as fast as rats. These monsters were everywhere! Her skin crawled as she began to realise she was trapped.

Suddenly Jude turned from the queue and walked swiftly away. Her neck jarred with shock. He had come to an abrupt halt. Another dream thief blocked his path.

There was a snarling voice. "Got a spring in yer step tonight? Yer got loads more than usual. A whole ton."

The creature's flickering shape was inches away. Ruth held her breath and kept stock still, her fingertip on her hood.

Jude stepped round his opponent and did not respond.

"Oi! I spoke to yer," the creature snapped.

"And I did not speak back . . ." Jude's voice oozed with darkness.

The creature's legs darted into view, blocking Jude's path, left, right, left again as Jude dodged him. Ruth's head hit against something hard and she stopped herself from crying out.

"Get away!" Jude growled. "Takin' this lot down m'self."

"Got yerself a right prize? Let's 'av a gander – yer always pick good 'uns." Jude's tormentor gave a little jig. "Oi 'ang on a minute – 'av yer got that girl's?"

He meant *her*! This must be the larger dream thief who had stood over her in her bedchamber.

"Yes . . . got her good and proper!" Jude virtually snarled back.

Had Jude tricked her? Did he see her as no more than a great prize?

All of a sudden the other creature seized the top of Jude's sack and yanked it so hard, it almost pulled from his grasp – but Jude held fast and would not let go, still bearing the true weight of the sack, which would give her away in an instant.

"Her dream's mine!" Jude growled.

Ruth swung back and forth, her insides liquid with fear. She pulled her hood as far down as it could possibly go, hiding her dream.

"Killjoy." The creature let go of the sack and moved away.

Every one of Ruth's muscles screamed out for release, as did her mind, too. Burst out of the sack! Run off the ship and down to Crowbury! But that was impossible – she wouldn't make two paces. She'd never escape. The ship was her prison. The plan she'd hatched with Jude was utter madness. What had possessed her to think she could ever stop the dream thieves, least of all on the one place where they were strongest?

Fear made her dizzy and faint. She couldn't catch her breath. Couldn't move. Sweat trickled down her skin. Swarming dream thieves crawling everywhere . . . A memory returned . . .

stumbling into a nest of spiders that ran up her legs. Her father had made it better and calmed her. He told her to think of something else while he gently dealt with them. She did this again now, willing herself to concentrate on her bearings. She made herself recall her father's descriptions of ships he had sailed. This was the deck. Perhaps that was the main mast. Ruth squinted upwards through a frayed hole, glimpsing stars beyond the ship's rigging, the mast piercing the sky as the ship swayed slowly from side to side. Its oily timbers grated as though poised to fly. She heard the creak of doors opening, very close.

Jude descended five or six steps down to a lower deck, bumping the sack once as they went. There was a sulphurous stench, and it was growing stronger . . .

27

The Shadow-Child

Jude took the final step and hesitated, sack swinging, before turning sharply right and walking down what seemed to be a passageway. Through the hole in the sack, Ruth found it impossibly difficult to see anything in the gloom. There were no voices – were they all working above deck? But less noise did not mean that nobody was there. Beyond the sound of blood pounding in her own ears there came a distant clicking, tapping, dripping and humming. Suddenly a door clicked open; the noises, smells and light amplified. Jude sidled through the door, closing it behind him. Light glared through the sacking. All was quiet. Even though there was no sign of imminent betrayal, she still was not convinced that Jude was going to do what they had planned. She held her breath. In moments, his true intentions would be revealed.

The sack was placed on solid ground, collapsing loose onto her skin. She didn't move a muscle. Then, above her head, there was the fumbling of hands . . . loosening the rope . . . opening the sack.

"Quick, hide!" Jude whispered fiercely.

At his words, Ruth felt tension go from her body. She started to edge out of the sack, casting around for Jude and more dream thieves. There he was, seemingly alone. His shadowy figure was turned away from her, preoccupied with something else. Surely this would not be happening if he had really planned to betray her?

Fixing her eyes on Jude and the room, she wriggled fully out of the sack, keeping the hood pulled over to hide her dream. Something cracked under her knee as she crawled. She bent to look. A dream halo, snapped in two. Dreams were scattered on the floor, spilling out from a sack beside her.

Black. Brittle. Dead.

Other lumpy sacks lay around that would surely be full of more halos. Ruth didn't dare move an inch. Breaking another person's dream was unthinkable – the opposite of what she had come to do!

"Hurry!" Jude jabbed his thumb at a table, under which she could hide.

But surrounded by these halos, she felt paralysed. She could not move. A scraping and a whoosh from above caused her to look up. A sack hurtled down the chute and thumped into her. A dream halo fell out and snapped on the floor. Reaching for the two halves, Ruth instinctively held them together as though they might join up, but they remained separate, like a broken plate with a large hole in the centre.

Whose dead, broken dream was this?

Ruth bit her lip. They were all coming from Crowbury. Had the creatures robbed dreams from further away – as far as Meg's?

"Go!"

She felt the pressure of Jude's shadowy hand ushering her beneath the table. She obeyed, moving beneath the shelter of the wood, hastily looking around the room as she pulled an empty sack over to cover her body.

Running down the centre of the room was a row of rectangular glass cabinets containing equipment, the likes of which she had never seen before. Attached to many of the walls were brown cupboards with words and numbers scribbled in white chalk over the doors. A mass of hessian sacks were strewn about. Yellow lamps hung along the walls, interspersed with a dozen or more clocks, their hands all set to the same time – the middle of the night. It was Crowbury's time. Though the hands stood in agreement, the variety of clocks was beyond anything she could have imagined, yet each had numerals all apart from one. This had magical lit-up numbers as though illuminated from behind. Another took the form of a miniature ship, intricately wrought in gold with a clock face attached to the mast. She'd noticed this kind of clock at Queen Elizabeth's Court . . . perhaps dreams were not the only thing they plundered. Ruth recalled what Jude had said about the ship visiting many different times . . . that made sense now, seeing the clocks.

Jude was darting around the cabinets, peering inside, trying to fathom their purpose. He felt his old Master Curiosity self stirring. Never before had he ventured beyond his quarters inside the ship. These cabinets were full of peculiar, fascinating contraptions and bubbling liquids. And scattered all around on the tables were tubes, dishes, pipes and peculiar glinting metal objects, which he picked up and examined.

The door opened. Instantly, Ruth shrank back. Two men strode into the room.

Humans? Dealing in dreams?

Papers rustled as the men busied themselves, discussing the contents in low voices. Anxiously, she looked for Jude and was relieved to see his body of shadows fold into the darkness behind a cabinet.

Unaware of the room's other occupants, the two men stood only a few steps from where Ruth was hiding. But they were so absorbed in their animated talk that she could watch.

They wore black shoes and long velvet breeches extended in straight lines up from their ankles – a fashion she had never seen before. She craned her neck as high as she dared. They wore waistcoats, one with a pocket watch on a chain, and also white ruffled shirts with a cloth tied at the neck. Wearing a tall hat made of silk, which seemed absurd on this ship, the older man sported a slither of a pointed beard and moustache twirled into points and a single eyeglass. He was fat, and stifled a burp with his hand and patted his stomach as the younger man spoke.

"So it's not actual magic, sir?"

The older man laughed, set down his hat and slicked back his grey hair.

"No. No spells, just science, but it's still *magical,* as such. You have so much to learn. Now, where were we?"

Ruth could not see what they were doing, but their instruments clicked away.

"That's it . . . steady does it . . . you place the dream here in the vacuum tube like this . . . flick that switch like that . . . yes . . . now turn the dial sharply towards the right – sharply now – expanding the dream so we can see it more clearly."

A click and a buzz were followed by a loud flash.

The older man giggled. Giddy with drink, Ruth thought.

"But it's still black!" The younger man seemed to object.

"And that's where the mirrors and light come in." The older one leaned in and spoke like a tutor to a child, patronising, and slightly drunk. "Once you have expanded the dream to its full size, you place your hands like this into the gloves inside the cabinet . . . release the clamp and move it along to the next stage of the operation. And that is?"

"The mirrors and light bit?" the younger man asked, weakly.

They shuffled further along the cabinets. Ruth could not see them so well.

"Yes, the optical figuring machine. We point the concentrated beam of light through the dream . . . like this . . ."

For all Ruth could understand, they could have been speaking in a foreign tongue, there were so many baffling words. Like her father's friends, Dee and Digges, these men were natural philosophers, but with a diabolical purpose, and from a time yet to come – a time that the dream thieves' ship had entered.

"And we use the crystal prism to refract the white light back into all the original colours . . . like that . . . then we flick this switch here . . . and . . ."

There was the crack of lightning, followed by a dull buzzing, which continued on. She heard a gasp.

"Hey presto!"

"Amazing!"

The older man laughed. "It's magnificent! Every time I see it I get a thrill – and I've done this dozens of times."

"Extraordinary." The younger man bent closer in. "You can see a child – hazy, but it's still a child alright – and all those images spinning around them!"

His description reminded Ruth of the child from the vision Godrick had shown her . . . but this felt like a perversion.

"Yes – that's information about their lives that I record for the captain."

He flicked another switch.

"It's life-size!"

"*Life*-size indeed!" the man laughed and rocked back on his heels. "In a manner of speaking, I suppose it is. And what we do, once we've got it all down, is flick that other switch there . . . and voilà! The child is turned into a shadow of itself."

Tension coursed through Ruth's body.

"Spooky!"

"It's just science. A dark holograph, a shadow-child."

Shadow-child? Ruth was desperate to see – but still their bodies blocked the view.

"What happens to the real child?"

"The – ahem – genius of my process has three key benefits. Number one: in the past, it required several thievings before despair started to work, and these damnable dreams do keep showing up! It takes time to kick the hope out of someone. Children are desperate to hold onto the last threads of hope, even when it looks useless."

Ruth clenched her fists.

"So my process here speeds things up a little. Before, we had to wait for hopelessness to take its course, when, eventually, a broken dream could create its own shadow-child with a little help from the creatures. This way, the results are instant and absolute."

"Excellent, sir."

"Number Two. We twist their dreams so the children do the opposite of what they had dreamt of, hurting themselves and other people. The captain, Lord Zephon, can rule over the chaos that ensues, although this is admittedly ad hoc at present. My invention quickens the process. It's wonderful. Zephon loves it – hence the bottles of the fine stuff to celebrate."

"And number three?"

"Well, it's that really," the older man blustered a little, wrong-footed at losing his own line of explanation. "Once I've perfected all this here, we won't just invert the dream – we can manipulate it to make someone do exactly what his lordship wants. We're not quite there yet, but it's within reach, once we've experimented on a few more children . . ."

"And the adults . . .?"

The scientist clapped his hands together. "Ex-actly, my son. That's the fourth benefit . . . The stakes get somewhat higher."

"Four benefits? Most impressive, sir."

"It's not as controlled as I'd like it to be, but I'm working on it. And you know what that they do with the shadow-children meanwhile."

"Yes."

Ruth was desperate to see this so-called shadow-child. Avoiding any more dream halos, she crawled along beneath the tables beside them, drawing closer, taking the sack with her for covering while the two men continued speaking.

"Anyhow, the whole point of getting an assistant – that's you, of course – is to increase productivity. You can carry on while I'm away helping Zephon, so we can work around the clock, so to speak." He gestured to the piles of sacks. "So many to get through. We need a filing system."

Ruth inched further along beneath the table until she finally saw the shadow-child.

A fragile, smoke-like figure of dark wisps stood in a large, round glass cabinet the height of a man. The faint figure sank to its knees. It looked frighteningly similar to a dream thief, except the way the little shadow-child moved could not be more different . . . cowed, terrified.

Ruth gulped. It could be the blacksmith's boy. Or Little Luce!

Both their dreams must have been stolen two nights ago – surely enough time for these macabre men to finger through the pile in the corner, and select his or her dream for this treatment.

She screwed up her eyes, searching for some distinguishing detail. The shadows thickened around the neck of the head, suggesting hair. And as the shadow-child turned to look about the cabinet, Ruth could see thickness continuing down the back – long hair, the same as Little Luce's!

The shadow-child looked at her own shadowy hands and limbs, confused, as if seeing them for the first time. She stood up again, moved up to the glass and pressed her little hands against it, realising she was imprisoned.

Suddenly, the wispy girl turned her head and looked directly at Ruth, who started in shock. For a few moments, they held one another's gaze. Seeing Ruth hidden beneath the table, the girl's shadowy eyes bulged.

It tore at Ruth's heart.

The men continued, oblivious to this moment of connection between the shadow-child and the stowaway.

"So, next, we activate the vacuum inside the tube on the right, here . . . like so . . . and yes – there it goes! Down the tube and into the Shadowlands."

The shadow-child was sucked feet-first down a broad tube that led out of the laboratory.

Arms flailing.

Hands grasping.

Mouth open hideously wide in a silent scream.

28

Even The Trees Cry Out

Suddenly the ship heaved to one side. All at once, the scientists, tables, equipment, Ruth – all were thrown violently. Her sack slipped off. Desperately, she grabbed the nearest table leg, yanked her knees up close, ensuring the edge of her nightgown and cape were still hidden from sight. Ruth's sack crashed into the scientist's shoes and he kicked it away.

"Good grief!" He shouted above the sounds of creaking wood. "I can't work like this! We can't start on another child now!"

What was happening? Was it the storm clouds?

The ship lurched back the other way, thrusting the men across the room and against the table just inches from Ruth. She was now jammed against the wall, with the dream halos bunched up behind her. The apparatus juddered and creaked as though it might tear apart, straining and buckling under the pressure. She hugged the table leg, afraid the ship would tilt back over once more.

The ship, Ruth realised, was unmooring from Crowbury! She broke out in a sweat.

"I can't work in these conditions," the scientist said. "The officer's mess beckons."

"So soon?"

"Fret not, anxious one," he said, stifling a burp. "We'll start again when they next drop anchor."

The two men made their way unsteadily towards the door as the ship creaked and tilted, and left the room.

Ruth stood up, holding onto the table, looking for Jude. She was beginning to panic. Their escape route was vanishing! They had planned, at the very least, to find the snatched blacksmith's boy, then Jude was to make two trips up and down the gangplank with sacks carrying first him and then Ruth. But that was now impossible.

The ship yawled and rolled. Somehow the cabinets were fixed and did not slide off their tables – all around the edges was a lip that just about stopped the loose instruments from falling on the floor.

Between two clocks on the far wall was a small porthole. Ruth rushed over and gripped its circular edge as she looked out.

Branches whipped past the glass. As the ship rose up the valley, tree tops lashed the vessel, as if the wood knew whom the ship was carrying and was fighting to hold on to her. Crowbury Hall! The ship rose high above the roofs and chimneys, sailing over Nurse and everyone else she knew, asleep below. It ascended the hill behind and glanced off the cairn of stones on the top.

Clouds flew past like scorching steam pumping from a kettle as the ship pitched to and fro. Crowbury was already far behind! Quickly, her eyes hunted the shadows for Jude. He was nowhere to be seen.

Outside, the view was changing, becoming nothing more than a blur, moving too fast to focus on anything. They were gathering speed, flying faster and faster. In seeking the lost children, neither she nor Jude had stopped to consider how she would ever return home should the ship leave too early – he'd thought they'd be moored for the night. Adam's words rang in her ears . . . *take care, you are making haste.*

Mechanical sounds broke into her thoughts. *Tick-tock, whizz, bang, whistle.* The clocks had manically sprung into action. Some hands leapt back and forth from 10 o'clock to 2 o'clock; others spun around continuously forwards or backwards in a demented fury. Pendulums swung madly, at odds with each other. She jumped as a squawking toy bird leapt out of the heart of a clock, nearly hitting her in the face. It was bedlam. Of course! It made sense to her now: time was being disrupted. They were not just leaving Crowbury, but her place in time, too.

How could she ever return – and to that precise moment?

She searched again for Jude's shadowy form and finally saw him. He was curled on the floor. She rushed over, clutching the table edges, to where he lay.

"Jude!!"

He hardly stirred.

"Jude! We're leaving!" She tried to rouse him, tried to grab him enough to shake him, but he did not respond. "Did you see it too – the shadow-child?"

He moved, but only to curl into a tighter ball. He barely seemed aware of her.

Ruth's heart beat loudly in her chest. Why was he not responding?

She shook him hard. "It could have been Little Luce! Where's she gone? What are these Shadowlands?"

Jude did not seem to hear her, and turned his head away.

She gritted her teeth. I've got to *do* something, she told herself.

She worked her way back over to the sacks of dreams, where so many blackened halos were scattered and sliding around the floor, treated by the dream thieves as if worthless – though they had been good enough to steal. She picked them up, grabbing handfuls of halos, opened her hunting bag and was about to place them in it when she saw *The Chronicles*. Thinking only to pack the bag well, she pulled it out and placed it to one side. Then a thought struck her. Quickly, she took *The Chronicles* in both hands. She pulled apart the leather binds and opened up the book, seeing for one second the inky words and figures leaping into action before being obscured by the explosion of dust from its heart.

Dust gathered in the air before her and she held her breath, full of awe. Tears brimmed.

Coughing and spluttering came from within the cloud . . .

"Adam!"

Dust billowed in her face. Could it be that even hidden by such darkness, the Guardian of Dreams had helped her? Adam had always been sent to aid her – first saving her horse from falling, then appearing in the library after seeing the dream thieves. And now here.

His form took shape. He smiled at Ruth, removed his hat from his head and shook it free of dust as he bowed low with his customary flourish.

"Gentle lady! Our conversation was somewhat curtailed, was it not?" Adam said pointedly, glancing around at the apparatus and furious clocks, while the room rocked from side to side. "Yet here I stand, at your bidding!"

He placed his feet apart to steady himself, unsuccessfully, for as the room tipped he promptly fell over with a crash. Ruth rushed to him and grabbed his hand, helping him up.

"Quiet, we need to be quiet," said Ruth, hushing him.

"Where on God's Earth are we?" he whispered. His eyes were now fixed on the cabinets and the equipment inside.

"We're trapped on the dream thieves' ship!" Her eyes were wide with urgency.

"The dream thieves!" Adam spat with disgust. "Those villainous hell-born harpies!" He looked around again, taking in what she had said, focusing on the apparatus. "Wait a moment . . . their *ship*?!" His eyes narrowed. "We had no idea such a thing existed!!"

"We are lost, Adam! And trapped! And they make shadow-children here, right here!" Her breath caught in her throat, desperate to tell him of all she had witnessed.

"*Shadow*-children?"

"I saw one being made inside there!" She indicated the cask where she had seen the terrified child, as light glanced off the empty glass. The entire mechanism creaked with every movement of the ship.

He nodded. "Never before have I heard of *shadow-children*."

"And we have left Crowbury – where we are going, I know not!"

"I see," he said more calmly, seeing the full force of her panic. He took her face in his dusty hands, cool on her skin.

"Gentle lady, do not give way to fear," he whispered.

Ruth shook her head, his presence nearly reducing her to tears.

Adam nodded. "I find it helps to focus one's mind on the facts, once we have established them." With a grimace he turned to the apparatus. "And besides, for me this is no worse than any other occasion. I rarely know where I shall appear next. Or whether I'll be given a warm welcome." He winked at Ruth and began to investigate the equipment.

The facts. It made Ruth think. What she had learned of this Lord Zephon was that he wanted information as well as the dreams. Surely, if they caught her, it would more likely mean interrogation than instant death. Would that give her a little chance of escape? Adam's words cut into her thoughts.

"So. They make shadow-children. You saw them make one inside here?"

Adam walked from one cabinet to the next, stroking his beard.

"Yes, but whatever you're doing, hurry Adam! The men could be back any minute. I heard them saying they can't work when the ship is moving."

Ruth glanced over her shoulder at the door. The clock hands were still spinning on the walls. She guessed they would stop once they reached the next destination.

"Once again dear lady, do not succumb to fear."

Methodically, using his thumb and forefinger, Adam examined every switch, valve, clamp, knob and tube that connected the cabinets . . . tweaking, twizzling, tapping and inspecting in minute detail.

"There is a girl I know from my house, Adam, Little Luce, and when I last saw her, she was so altered that I thought at the time she was like a shadow of herself! A *shadow*! A shadow-child!! I think it was she who I saw before in that cabinet, when the scientists made one. I think the shadow-child was Little Luce!"

Adam glanced up "I hope you are incorrect, gentle lady."

On Ruth gabbled, following Adam around the cabinets, desperate to share everything she knew before the scientists returned. "Even if it was not Little Luce, the shadow-child may have been from my town – they must have been using a dream from Crowbury to make it. And do you remember you told me that some people in power worked with the dream thieves?"

Adam nodded.

"This, here, is part of that scheme, Adam. The . . . the 'scientists' as they called themselves said they could change dreams to make people do as they want."

Adam let out a "Whoo!!" and sped up his analysis of the equipment.

"It all makes sense," he said. "We thought that hopelessness changed behaviour, numbing the soul. But they use this contraption to actively pervert the Guardian's dreams. It does seem to be some kind of optical figuring machine . . . fascinating . . . surprisingly clever . . . a research prototype perhaps."

Ruth could not comprehend his words nor did she ask him to explain. Her head was already too full. She had to tell him more.

"They also said once they had perfected controlling children, they would start on older people."

"Did they now?"

"It makes me think of my stepmother – she must have had her own dreams stolen."

"Hmm. They may intend to make more machines to increase productivity – I would. The Guardian will want to know all this. And there may be experiments in progress, perhaps on other ships." Adam was scrutinising the calculations scribbled in white chalk on the cupboard doors.

"What? More ships of thieves?"

He paused suddenly, turned to Ruth and looked her in the eye. "Speaking of ships, how did you come to be on this one?"

"I wanted to rescue the lost children from Crowbury! But if they're already shadow-children, how can I tell one apart from the rest? That shadow-child looked like a dark ghost, like the dream thieves, but different. Oh, I should not have come . . ."

"Still, answer me, gentle lady. How did you come to be on this ship – were you captured?"

"It was Master Curiosity – I found him again and he agreed to help me," Ruth hurriedly confessed.

"What?!" Adam swallowed hard. He focused on her again. "So *that* is why you dispensed with me. You clotpole!" Adam was turning red with anger. "And now you are trapped on this ship! Venomous dog, that dream thief, and you believed him! I told you, I told you not to–"

"I did, Adam," Ruth cut in, piqued. "I believed him. *Yes*, he is a dream thief – or *was* a dream thief – but he *really* was once a boy, and it was *him* – Jude – the boy whose dream you picked out from The Chronicles – the one you placed in my head! He used to be the candle-maker's lad and he knew my grandfather. He had hopes and dreams but terrible things happened. You saw his blackened dream! After seeing you, I went to the old candle shop because I thought that he might go there – and he did! He promised to help me find the lost children."

Adam stared at her, eyes wide, his hand gripping the table.

"'Tis true!" she continued, seeing he was not convinced. "Because he had been stolen away himself. Adam, my own dreams have been full of black snow and an ice boy. And all along my dream was about Jude, the dream thief. Many threads connect us. The Guardian showed me through my dreams."

Adam took off his hat. His face was less red now, and he took one or two breaths, ran his fingers through his hair. "Where is this dream thief now?"

"There!" Ruth pointed to the spot where Jude lay, still curled in a ball.

"What???!!! Here?!" Adam recoiled. "I have never seen one of those vile creatures!" He pulled a dagger from a sheath on his belt.

"Put that away! He's no danger, I swear it."

Adam pirouetted, waving his dagger around, duelling like a swordsman before an invisible foe. "Where is he?"

"I told you, you do not need that. I cannot rouse him. He is lying there, in the shadows."

Adam followed her finger, and sucked in his cheeks. He glanced at Ruth.

"He cannot harm you now," she said.

He put away the dagger and picked up instead a long glass rod from the mess on the table, approaching the darkened place where Jude lay. He prodded around the shadows.

"Where is the damn thing?"

Ruth saw Jude roll over. She hoped that Adam's vigorous swiping with the rod would bring him round.

"Nothing's here."

"But he is there! You are touching him!" Ruth was adamant. She felt Adam's eyes turn upon her, watching her watching Jude.

"Gentle lady. This confirms what we have always suspected. We are unable to see dream thieves. They are creatures of diabolical darkness . . . and if we see *nothing* then we know not when we should see *anything*." He poked the shadowy place again. "But we can sense evil," he added as if to himself. "So why can I not sense him?"

"Because he is no longer evil!"

Adam paused, rubbing his beard.

"So tired . . ." Jude murmured.

Adam started; Ruth looked at him sharply.

"You heard him!"

"I heard something . . . above the sounds of those clocks, as if the air had trembled."

"Good! You see, he is there!"

"This is not what I would have expected of those vile creatures."

Adam was at it again with the glass rod. Ruth could see Jude rolling back over.

"I do not understand why he will not wake up!" Ruth said. "He must have seen them make the shadow-child – why doesn't he want to help?"

"*If* you *are* correct, and he has undergone some manner of conversion, in watching the making of a shadow-child, he may have entered a state of mind called *cognitive dissonance*."

"Pardon?"

"A term from science of the future. When one's beliefs are challenged to the point of collapse, it can cause deep distress and exhaustion."

Adam's words made perfect sense. She stared at this wretched creature who had once been a boy, and screwed up her eyes in frustration. That turnaround outside the candle-maker's had been too fast and too easy. Perhaps she had been right to worry as they were touched by the waves of evil flowing off the ship. But now, having witnessed the creation of a shadow-child, he was undone. All those years of thieving had stitched him up into an evil place, yet seeing the shadow-child was unravelling all that hope-hating. What she didn't know, of course, was whether Jude had first become a shadow-child before he became a dream thief – or whether it had happened all at once. He may not even know himself.

After a few moments, Jude's breaths slowed to a steady pace and his limbs uncurled a little.

"I think he may be sleeping," she whispered.

"Hmm. And I am wondering."

He bounded over to *The Chronicles* and flicked rapidly through the pages. When he found what he was searching for, he removed the pincers from his pocket and, inching the metal mouth closer, he pinched the edge of a dream, twisted it and extracted it from the book. It was smaller than his fingertip. Shielding the little halo, he shambled his way over to the optical figuring machine. Frowning with concentration, he released brass clasps along one particular cabinet and opened the glass door. Ruth watched intently. Looking greedily at the apparatus within, Adam clamped the dream in place. It pulsed light then dark then light, over and over again. He flicked a switch. A bright beam passed through the dream, causing it to swell. The tiny prism dissolved the darkness of the dream, refracting white light into rainbow colours.

"Careful, Adam!" said Ruth quickly, not forgetting what had happened when the so-called scientists used this equipment.

Adam held up his left hand, as if to acknowledge her caution, not taking his eyes off the dream halo for one moment. Still swelling, the dream started spinning to white. It rocked with the motion of the ship. Ruth held her breath, and glanced up at the clocks with their demented hands. Adam flicked another switch and swung open the glass door as the beam of light faded. With great delicacy, he touched the edge of the rainbow and lifted it up and out of the apparatus, removing it from the cabinet with both hands. He turned. Ruth gasped, suddenly understanding what Adam was about to do. He carried it carefully to the place where Jude lay, and knelt down.

"Where is his head? Guide my hands."

Ruth knelt and directed Adam's hands to the crown of Jude's head.

"There, just there," she said. "That's right, his forehead is this way."

Adam released the halo, checking with Ruth that the dream was placed just where it should be, adjusting the angle and position. Jude's shadowy body locked onto the dream. Adam slowly released his hands from the halo, hardly daring to draw back.

Slowly, slowly, the colours began to blur and released a flare of light; Adam nodded to himself and smiled. Chink by chink, the dream halo settled, arcs and whorls of colour turning around Jude's head.

Ruth could not stop herself crying out.

"Jude is dreaming!"

29

The Golden Box of Dreams

"Well I never!"

Adam stared at the dream, the halo moving steadily over Jude's faint head. He removed his hat, placed it on the floor and scratched his head vigorously.

"This should be impossible!"

Ruth held her breath as Jude's dream grew ever stronger with each moment. It pulsed light, building up colour and illuminating Jude's body of shadows.

"I see him now . . . an outline of a creature . . . like a man, but not."

Adam sat back on his heels, taking in his first sight of a dream thief.

But Ruth's eyes were on the dream, not the sleeper. Never before had she seen such beautiful colours, which were more vivid than anything she had ever witnessed. They were like exquisite stained glass, effervescent pigment. Midnight blue arose to iridescent emerald green, through the colour of sand, coral and rubies. Faster and faster the colours of Jude's dream streamed until they melted together, blending into pure shining white.

"I *do* see the creature," Adam said, dazed, scratching his head.

The halo pulsed, ever stronger, over the Jude's shadowy body, highlighting every limb.

"He *was* a human," Adam said, astonished. "Some vestige of his soul must have remained. This would be inconceivable, otherwise."

He met her eyes. She saw the dawning of a terrible realisation.

"I know," she said. "How many more times has this happened . . ."

He nodded, his eyes turning back to Jude.

"So could you do this for shadow-children?" Ruth asked, thinking of Little Luce. "Or for any other dream thieves who were once human, too?"

Adam shook his head.

Of course, restoring other dreams was out of the question. Even if Ruth found the shadow-children, how would they ever pair up the faint creatures with their real counterparts in *The Chronicles*? Little Luce's dream would not even be in this volume. And who was to say when other shadow-children had lived? As for finding out whether other dream thieves had once been human . . . No. Ruth and Jude shared a unique link. Surely this process could never be replicated. She touched Jude's shoulder and his dreamlight radiated over her hand and arm.

She glanced at Adam. His eyes were ablaze. He leapt up and set to, his fingers a blur of activity. Switches were broken. Fine glass tubes snapped. Using the broken glass, he cut through the soft piping connecting one section to another. He worked methodically, quietly and with total concentration. There was nothing theatrical about him now as he moved around, keeping himself steady on the swaying floor. He disappeared around the back of another section of the diabolical machine. Ruth heard the cracks and tinkles as he systematically tackled the rest, sabotaging the machine, but in a subtle way to give Ruth the greatest chance of escape before this was discovered. Hampering the dream thieves was at least one thing they could do. He found a piece of chalk and carefully rubbed out some numbers from the calculations, adding different numbers instead.

Finally, Adam reappeared at the end of the machine beside Ruth and the sleeping Jude. In his hand was the large crystal prism that had channelled light into the dream.

"Best take this with me," he said, tucking it inside his pocket.

Suddenly the ship juddered. Were they slowing down? The spinning clock hands on the walls changed their pace.

"You *must* find a way off," Adam said. "And this time you *must* do as I say! I cannot help you for I am blind to the dream thieves – I would only put you in greater danger! You must not be captured or leave The Chronicles here."

"But the Crowbury children!"

Adam gripped her shoulder. "Leave them. Get off the ship. You cannot let the dream thieves get hold of The Chronicles."

Ruth nodded. Even in her stubbornness she knew that letting *The Chronicles* fall into the wrong hands was unthinkable. It did not matter that the dreams were from past times – they could still harvest hundreds of souls. She already knew this, but now she felt the full force of it. In trying to rescue the lost children, she had set herself a hopeless task and endangered so much. What had she been thinking?

"Good sir," Ruth said quickly, and the corner of her mouth twitched in a smile of farewell as she picked up *The Chronicles*, holding it open. Adam nodded. Ruth knew what she had to do. She closed the book. Adam disappeared in a puff of dust. For a moment she stood, watching the space he had just occupied.

She lifted the flap of her bag and placed *The Chronicles* beside the vial of tears, feeling the weight of responsibility, slinging it across her body beneath her cape in what she hoped was not a useless attempt to keep it safe. She looked around the laboratory.

The clocks were still moving. Jude was still sleeping.

Kneeling down, she shook him roughly, but he was too deeply asleep to come round. Should she wait and hide there with him until he awoke? Soon those men and others could be back. She could not decide a thing.

In trying to help the frozen boy, she had trapped herself.

Ruth shivered, her hand on her hunting bag. One thing was clear. When the scientists returned, they would see Jude's shining dream – and what would they do to him, a dreaming dream thief! Unimaginable! Seizing an empty sack, she laid it over Jude's head, covered his halo and gingerly tucked it under his shadows. His legs poked out. She hoped this was enough to hide him.

She glanced over at the sabotaged equipment. At least no more shadow-children could be made for now.

Ruth took one last look at the sleeping Jude. She lifted the hood of her cape to hide her own halo of light and made her way towards the door. Her hand to the wood, she listened carefully, opened it a fraction, and peered out.

The sulphurous stench filled her nostrils. Timbers creaked and groaned, reverberating down the passageway.

To her left, a dismal glow came from two lamps on the wall, but it was enough to see when a dream thief was coming. There were voices. Muffled. Behind a door, perhaps? She must take her chance and leave while the corridor seemed empty. But which way should she go?

To her right, steps led up to a door – perhaps the route Jude had taken. If so, it would lead to the top deck but that would be crawling with dream thieves. Beyond the steps, the passageway was dark – too dark to be safe.

The doors to her left lined the passageway like sentries. The one at the end was fringed with light. Each door had a spyhole. She hesitated. Anyone inside might see her dreamlight if she put her eye to it – how could she see a way out? But with light glowing from the spyhole of the brightest room, she'd be safer to look.

Closing the door to the laboratory with a quiet click, she inched her way along the walls, fingers first, telling herself to hurry – at any moment, a dream thief could appear.

She ducked past the first doorway, then the second, and was almost at that end of the passageway when she heard voices from a room on the other side. She froze. There was the scrape of a chair across floorboards. Sudden cat-calls, jeers and shouts, and the sound of dice hitting the floor. A game?!

Melting with fright, she forced herself to move along. She had to get away!

Coils of rope and barrels were scattered around where the passage was broader. Quickly she checked the remainder of the corridor around the corner. It led to dark stairs beyond – to lower decks, she thought.

Returning to the door, she put her eye to the bright shining spyhole, searching for a way out.

At first, seeing was impossible. Then her eyes adjusted. Through the distorting circle of glass, the room appeared huge and distant. No creature was in her line of sight – but that did not mean that none were there. Her eyes hunted for windows. But what she saw shocked her.

Dreamlight was streaming from a row of halos, each suspended inside its own small glass box with gold edges, turning slowly like trapped stars. These dreams were valued. It was like some ghoulish, evil Cabinet of Curiosities.

There was another source of light. She craned to see from the spyhole. An Armillary Sphere! Like her own, save for the Sun instead of Earth at its centre – which Adam had said was correct. And this Sun was shining . . . a golden orb. In fact, it was more than shining. She could sense its force, pulsing power, driving the rotating rings of planets and stars by itself. Just as these monsters had built that machine to manipulate dreams, had they bastard-ised this sphere to manipulate time itself? This could be how they jumped between moments and places.

Scattered over an ornate wooden table were charts, held down by navigational instruments. Far from an escape route, this place looked like a captain's cabin.

A dark figure flitted across her line of sight.

She recoiled, stepped backwards and almost lost her footing on the ropes as a door creaked open nearby – the door to the deck! A claw-like foot of rippling black flames extended down to the top step.

30

Sagazan

Ruth flattened herself against the wall, saw the barrels and threw herself behind them, pulling an empty sack over herself, checking her hood was still hiding her dream. The dream thief descended. Voices grew louder.

Through a sliver of a gap between barrels, there was a view of the passageway. The creature of dark shadow flames towered over a man. They were walking her way.

The man's eyes darted this way and that. They were shot through with red veins like mackerel, matching a veiny bulbous nose and large cheeks. He daubed his sweaty forehead with a lace-edged handkerchief – a man of wealth, obviously. And he looked strangely familiar. Ruth peered more closely. He had short, greying, curly hair and a pointed beard, peppered with grey. He pulled back a fur cloak and, like a courtier, rested his hand on his hip, exposing a doublet and hose made of silk – shimmering in this half-light like her stepmother's dresses. Ruth *had* seen the man before, she was sure of it.

The courtier, pompous, frustrated, was barely restraining himself from shouting at the dream thief, which was absurd, as though he was clueless about the dangers he faced. Covering the man's head was a soft cap so she couldn't see his dream – whether it was still coloured or black as hell and under the dream thieves' control.

The courtier gestured towards the captain's cabin. "Sagazan, you must see it from our point of view," he said. "Zephon has breached his end of our agreement – despite all we have paid! And we've left Crowbury!"

Ruth felt a prickle of shock.

The dream thief called Sagazan stopped walking, and eyeballed the courtier. "And I said to tell yer Mister Devereux that *Lord* Zephon doesn't take nicely to anyone telling 'im what to do!"

The courtier held out his hands in exasperation. "Regardless of his agreement, and all that gold?"

"Well," Sagazan answered, "it boils down to 'ow much yer value what he does."

"Zephon has bled us dry!"

"That so?" The dream thief looked down and fingered the ermine fur collar of the courtier's cloak. "See, we are wondering how much yer Mister Devereux of Essex really values Lizzie's dream?"

"Her Majesty Queen Elizabeth's dream? The crown of England? It is of inestimable value!"

Despite herself, Ruth gasped. Queen Elizabeth's dream! Ruth recalled the treasured dreams held in those fine cases in the captain's cabin – they were kept to be sold to the highest bidder.

"Inestimable value, eh? How much is that?" said Sagazan, toying with the courtier.

Even Ruth could see that the dream thieves had no intention of keeping their word, no matter how much this courtier and Devereux paid up.

Sagazan was playing with the man, and the man could not see it.

"But it is only of value once my master has it. And Zephon has taken all the gold. It's been one broken promise after another," he said.

The courtier moved closer towards the captain's cabin – closer to where Ruth was hiding – and then stumbled over the coiled ropes and corrected himself. He could have fallen so close to her! Ruth shifted behind the barrels.

"Taken all yer gold?" The dream thief positioned himself between the courtier and the door. "I think yer got more – yer wouldn't come all the way up 'ere from London empty-handed. Remember what that dream means: control of the Queen . . . yer could convert her Catholic . . . marry her off to Spain . . ." The dream thief put its shadowy hand on the man's arm and leant in close. "Turn her stupid and seize the throne yerself."

Ruth watched the man's face turn purple with disgust at seeing the dream thief's hand on his sleeve. He shrugged it off.

"You ain't the only ones who're after it," Sagazan added with a smirk.

Immediately the man's expression changed to one of desperation, urgency.

"Yes . . ." the courtier muttered. "There was a . . . shipwreck or two and we secured other funds. Here." He pulled out a soft moneybag from his cloak and held it open as the dream thief peered inside. "They're Moroccan, Venetian – coins and ducats . . . ingots and jewellery – all solid gold."

Sagazan took it, lifting it up high. "I'll weigh it."

The courtier closed his eyes and nodded, resigned.

Sagazan whistled and a small shadowy figure – the height of a small child – appeared from the room with the players, carrying a set of scales and weights. Tipping the pouch, the contents slithered through its fingers into the scales. The small creature added and removed weights to the counter scale, balancing it out until the correct amount had been found. Sagazan crouched low and scoured through the treasure. He dipped his fingers inside the pile and pulled out a large golden coin, and stood up, lifting it high until it caught the light from the wall lamp, glinting in the gloom.

"Ha! A shiny English coin with Lizzie's head on it! God save the Queen – ha!"

And then something happened that made Ruth's blood run cold, for she sensed there was more to come. The courtier was completely misreading the whole situation. The dream thief blew on the coin and it flared red-hot. He tossed it to the courtier who caught the gold but instantly dropped it.

"Ow!" The courtier inspected his burnt fingers.

The dream thief paused, inclining its head to one side as he eyeballed the courtier, its black eyes gleaming. "Thing is, ain't enough gold."

"It's a small fortune!" The courtier's face was the colour of beetroot.

"Wait 'ere." Sagazan poured the gold back into the moneybag and entered the captain's cabin, closing and locking the door behind him.

The man tried to follow Sagazan, rattling the handle, but it would not open, so he peered eagerly through the spyhole, just as Ruth had done earlier.

Minutes passed.

The man loosened his cloak and wiped sweat off his forehead, which re-formed in beads as fast as he could wipe it away. He fished around in his pocket. Ruth started. The way the courtier found his pocket watch, flicked it open and checked the time in one swift movement reminded her so strongly of her father.

Should she seize her chance? Speak to this man?

She held her breath.

No. She could never trust a human with such an agenda.

There was the sound of a key turning in a lock and Sagazan returned with empty hands.

"Our lord's too busy, he won't see yer."

"But my gold!" the courtier blustered, staring at the dream thief's empty hands.

"What gold?" Laughing, the dream thief showed his empty palms, mocking him. "Anyway, he likes the look of Spanish gold better."

"You're giving her dream to the Spaniards!! But you've taken everything!"

"Not quite everything . . ." The dream thief spoke these words more slowly.

"I cannot return to Devereux with nothing!"

The dream thief laughed. He couldn't have cared less.

"But our deal! I demand to see Zephon myself!"

"Nah! He can't be bothered wiv yer."

"Outrageous!"

The courtier barged towards the door and as he did so, Sagazan's flame-like muscles rippled, instantly becoming more like solid flesh than shadow, barring the way.

"You're a nobody! Let me through!" the courtier shouted.

The dream thief pulled him around by his collar and pinned him to the wall by his throat.

"I 'aint *nobody*," Sagazan sneered, slowly. "I 'av a name and it is Sagazan."

The man struggled. But Sagazan had him pinned.

"Oh by the way," he said casually, "I saw yer precious little son the other night . . ."

The man stopped struggling as the dream thief's words sank in.

". . . And now 'e's got a loverly lickle black dream."

"You're evil!" The man made a grab for the dream thief's neck but the creature blocked him with his arm.

"Yer'll curse the day of 'is birth now. He'll give yer hell." Sagazan laughed. "Evil is my good. And I do good with a passion."

Black flames leapt from his mouth, searing through the courtier's clothing.

His cry rose to a scream as his flesh began to burn.

Sagazan plunged his hand deep inside the man's chest and pulled out bleeding strings of entrails. He yanked the guts higher and looped them around courtier's neck as he grasped at his insides in a futile attempt to hold his body together.

Ruth's stomach churned. Vomit rose in her throat but she could not tear her eyes away.

"Heh! A frilly red sash around yer throat to match yer silks!"

Blood poured down the man's waistcoat and over his breeches. His organs spilled out. His face was an agonised scream, splitting the air.

Sagazan regarded him coolly then pulled the courtier's entrails tight around his neck as if to strangle him. Finally, he let out an inferno of fire from his mouth, torching the man from head to toe.

Ruth's body trembled violently as she watched the courtier's clothes burn first, then his flesh, exposing his skull with his jaw wide open in a final gurgle. His flailing skeleton burned ferociously, until there was nothing left but a pile of ash.

Sagazan dusted himself off, shook his rippling muscles of black fire in a display of dominance, and then reverted back to his fainter shadowy form. He poked his head around Lord Zephon's door.

"Job done, your Lordship."

Ruth heard a murmur in reply. Zephon, the ship's captain. His voice was dark and low. A coldness wrapped around her.

These creatures were evil incarnate.

Sagazan nodded, clicked the door shut and took a step down the passageway as if to leave. But then he paused, glanced back over his shoulder in the direction of the barrels where Ruth was hiding.

He bent down. He grabbed the piles of rope which the courtier had tripped over, crossed the passageway to the second room along, opened the door – a store cupboard – and threw the ropes inside. Sagazan sniffed the air once, twice. Then he stalked back to the stairs and went above deck.

31

Trapped

Terrified, Ruth raised herself up, checking this way and that, and clutching the sack and hunting bag to her chest, bolted for the store cupboard. She slid inside, leaned against the door and scanned the room.

Angular shadows creaked with the ship from top to bottom, side to side. A porthole beyond showed rushing blackness outside. Inside, in front of her, lay the rope flung in by Sagazan. There were piles of boxes that had long since fallen over. A filing cabinet rested on its side, empty drawers open. A broken stepladder had fallen across it. Two carcasses of birds lay side by side, their feathers still intact: they had clearly been shut in the room, starved to death. Everything was smothered in grey dust and old bird droppings.

There was no sense of a dream thief lurking in here.

She clambered through the clutter to the porthole, fumbled around for a latch and pulled fiercely at its edges, but it was sealed as tight as a coffin lid. She pulled again. Still nothing. Even if it did open, she'd never be small enough to crawl through. And outside there was nothing but rushing darkness. She stood there, stifling a cry of frustration.

She was completely trapped. Those scientists would discover the sabotage soon. It was only a matter of time.

If they did not find her, she would waste away like those birds.

The strength drained out of her and she sunk to her knees, covering herself with the sack.

No sooner had she pulled the sack over her head than she heard the quiet but distinct click of the door handle. Every muscle tensed and she shrank to a small ball beneath the sack, gripping her legs. She hardly dared breathe. She listened.

Boxes were being lifted and moved. A dream thief was searching the store.

Footsteps came closer, closer.

She saw the sack was not covering all of her – the edge of her boot was showing.

The sack was swept away.

Had she been standing, her legs would have buckled.

As he looked down at her, a grin spread across his face from ear to ear.

"'Tis I."

Human. A young lad. He stood over her, his eyes burning bright. He wore a ragged tunic and breeches. And a hat: Adam's hat.

"'Tis me! Jude!"

Uncomprehending, her mind raced. She started to take this in. Her hand flew to her mouth. Jude.

Human Jude?

The boy reached out a hand towards her. That hand. It was an echo of her old black snow dream . . . the times she had awoken in her bed in Crowbury when the freezing boy was reaching out and pleading for help. But this boy, this boy *Jude*, was not asking for help. He was offering it.

Slowly, she lifted her fingers towards him, and his hand – so solid, so warm – grabbed hers. As he pulled her to her feet, she felt the weight of his body counterbalance her own. She was so dizzy and light, she might just drift away.

Jude stood there, beaming. He lifted his hat and bowed before her, revealing the dream halo that Adam had re-created. Spinning bright. Full of colour and life and light.

Now Jude reached up again, this time towards her head. She watched warily as he pulled her hood back, so tenderly, revealing her own dream. It pulsed with light, as if in response to his. His eyes shone, reflecting her dreamlight. Hazel eyes. Not dream thief-black. An echo of the moment they first met.

She touched his arm through his tunic, feeling flesh beneath thin material.

The act of restoring Jude's dream had been so profound, it had not just created hope, but bone and sinew, flesh and blood. The dream thief had vanished.

Tears sprang to her eyes.

"Oh Jude!" Ruth gulped.

She reached out and hugged him, aware of the body beneath her hands and arms, his head with his lank brown hair pressing into her shoulder. The smell of the candle-maker's shop was upon him, but she did not care.

Jude reached around her, hugging her tight, feeling the warmth of her trembling body as she barely suppressed sobs. The last time he had been this close to a human, he had stolen her dream. But now it could not be more different. Their dreams were almost locked together. Her disbelief, followed by astonishment at his physical body had made the transformation more real to him. He gripped her cape. He could feel again – cloth, her hair falling on his shoulder as they held each other. He took a deep breath, felt air fill his lungs. He dug his toes into his shoes, and flexed his thighs, felt the strength in his legs.

She let go and took in the sight of this real boy, the boy who had haunted her every time she had fallen asleep.

Jude dug his hands into his pockets. "I didn't mean to scare you."

She nodded.

"See," he continued, "I wasn't sure you was in here, but you couldn't have got far. I couldn't shout out . . ."

They faced such peril, yet hope shone from his eyes. The whole dream of black snow came flooding back and she trembled with the sense of its importance. Far from an omen, it was like a prophecy that had come good. Now, no black shadows swarmed around Jude. Evil had shed itself like a snakeskin. Deep down, all along, he was still the true Jude.

"*Non Sine Sole Iris*," she muttered, as he pulled her towards the door. The pebble of peace was dropping inside her once again, the same peace she had experienced upon meeting Godrick but doubly so, the ripples of calm at odds with the terror of the ship.

Jude looked back at her quizzically.

No Rainbow Without Sun. How could she begin to explain it to him? All she knew was that whatever happened next – if they never escaped – then at least this one thing made sense. A thought struck her.

"Jude, tell me . . . in the laboratory . . . when you were sleeping . . ."

"Er, yeh?"

"Of what did you dream?"

His face filled with amazement at the memory.

"'Twas a kind of bliss! I dreamt of wrong things being set right, of things being made fair, saying sorry . . ." He drifted away for a moment, then his eyes came into focus, staring at the darkness outside behind Ruth. "See, Ruth, look."

The ship was slowing down. Everything in the store was thrown forwards. Ruth hung on to the porthole, and Jude held on to her.

They turned to look at the night outside, gripping on to the porthole as the angle of descent became sharper. Moments later, the ship levelled out. It was still dark – too dark to see with the reflections from their dreams. Jude replaced his hat and lifted up Ruth's hood for her. He righted a box and stepped on it to see out more easily.

They were in some new earthly place and time. The ship was skirting around a series of flat low buildings, only one storey high. There were dozens of them. Thick smoke belched out of two chimneys. Encircling all was a tall, thin fence made of wire, and a forest beyond. A tall watchtower stabbed the sky. Regular as clockwork, piercing white beams of light would sweep over this complex, so bright that nothing earthly could escape its glare.

Slowly, silently, unseen, the ship sank lower until Ruth thought they would glance off the rooftops. Small windows beckoned, lower still – and soon, she and Jude might be able to see through them.

"We might never be able to go back to Crowbury – or not in the same moment that we left," Ruth said quietly, not tearing her eyes from the scene before her.

"P'raps . . . but I'll try and think . . ." His voice tailed away as he gripped the side of the porthole even tighter. He just stared and stared through the glass, not with the eyes of a dream thief, but of a boy.

She glanced at his fingers. Long ago, they had crafted candles in the workshop in Crowbury and presented her beloved old family curiosities to the world. Those fingers must have at some time clasped her grandfather's hand. Those eyes would have seen him. Those ears would have heard his voice – she might never even hear her own father's voice again.

Down below them, the people wore ragged, striped clothes. Woven upon many shirts was a large cloth star, faint yellow, the colour picked out in the weak moonlight and sweeping searching lights that momentarily passed over. These people were shaven-headed and half-starved.

Was this a prison? Or a madhouse?

Some of the doors in the flat low buildings were open and they could see inside. People were slumped asleep on stacked wooden platforms. A few others were awake. Three spoke furtively in the corner of one room. Two others comforted each other, holding close. Another sat upright, eyes closed, muttering a prayer. And all the time still turning around the heads of those still sleeping were their dreams. Faint white. Their precious lifelines to hope.

None reacted as though they had seen the ship as it glided silently down the row of buildings. They sailed higher again, avoiding the chimneys. Jude pointed to a huge pile of carcasses stacked high, a morass of gangly limbs.

"Deer?" he whispered.

But they both knew that these were human. Had there been a plague?

Smoke from the chimneys obscured their view, and when it cleared they were moving above a large courtyard at the edge of this grim place. Exiting a long carriage with wheels – but no horses – trailed a line of raggedy people. Men and women of all ages carried little ones asleep, bundled in coats and shawls. Older children walked, clutching a parent's hand or holding onto one another. Every face was drawn with fear. They dragged their feet as they walked into the compound, as if each step was taken in dread. Roughly, soldiers separated the men into a parallel line and directed old people and those struggling to walk into a third line, and their tears and distress as they parted made it perfectly clear that these were families, loving families, being forcibly separated.

One soldier barked commands to a mother who clung to her crippled daughter.

Turning around the soldier's head was a black, black dream.

She remembered the old blackness of Jude's dream. The dream thieves could be controlling this man. Ruth looked at Jude.

He held onto the porthole so tightly, his knuckles were white.

Pleading and begging, the mother refused to let go of her daughter. But the soldier persisted, shouting his commands. The mother was so desperate she jumped up and scratched the soldier's face. The soldier whipped out his revolver and shot both the mother and her child. Their bodies dropped to the ground.

People all around flinched but hardly dared move. Fingers clutched at those closest, holding tighter still.

The ship came to a stop. The dream thieves roared as they streamed off the ship and scattered throughout the camp. Working as an army, they swarmed from hut to hut. It all seemed to take place in the space of one breath. Hundreds of dreams severed from these poor souls.

Ruth could no longer bear to look. She turned away. Jude was pale with fear.

He bent double and retched, holding his stomach as he vomited. With the back of his hand, he quickly wiped his mouth, and felt the light pressure of Ruth's hand on his back. He stood up, seeing such emotion in her eyes. But how could this girl feel anything for him, given everything he had done?

"I've been there before," he murmured, ashamed. "Officers'll come up 'ere next – guests for Zephon. We 'av to get away."

Jude's eyes darted towards the door.

32

The Shadowlands

Taking Ruth by the hand, Jude led her back into the corridor, constantly looking around for Zephon and the dream thieves.

Not looking down, his stepped into the pile of ash that once was the courtier.

Adam's hat was firmly covering his head; her cape hood, her own dream.

Pulling her towards the laboratory, he checked at the door and turned the handle.

She reached out to stop him.

"The scientists!" Her eyes were wide.

Jude shook his head. He'd heard nothing from inside.

"They'll be back any moment," she said in a whisper, throwing another glance over her shoulder.

"We'll 'av gone," Jude countered, quietly.

She did not know what he meant but followed him inside.

He rushed to the far side of the room, to the tall round glass cabinet where she had seen the shadow-child.

"Hurry!" Jude whispered.

His hands were searching the surface of the rounded glass, looking for a way in. Not finding one, he went around the back, to a vast pipe that exited the cabinet and snaked away through the juncture between the wall and floor timbers. It was the height of a small child and double the width of his torso. He pressed the casing with his hands – it gave and flexed.

"This'll do," he said, "better than smashing the glass. It'll gi' us a chance."

He pulled a table over, indicating to Ruth to help him.

"Push it up against the wall, see, so it hides the pipe."

Quickly, he wrapped his hand around some sacking and found a jagged glass pipette, broken by Adam when he sabotaged the equipment. Jude crouched under the table and cut through into the huge diameter of the pipe, leaving the bottom third intact.

"This'll take us off the ship, away to the Shadowlands," Jude said as he forced the jagged sides apart – wide enough for a body.

Instantly, she felt air being sucked down into the yawning chasm . . . the darkness that had sucked away the shadow-child with silent screams. This did not feel like escaping. This felt like falling deeper into a trap. She half-sobbed and looked away.

"'Tis the only way off," he said.

She shook her head, speechless.

"'Tis our only escape!"

Seeing she would not move, Jude busied himself with getting his feet and legs inside, then shuffled his whole body into the tube, holding on tight to Adam's hat.

"Follow me!"

He lowered his body vertically as the pipe abruptly turned down into the ship. His head and hat disappeared, arms and hands gripping the jagged edge of the pipe. He held out his hand to her – the hand of human flesh that she had helped to re-create.

She grabbed his fingers.

"C'mon!" His whisper echoed from inside the pipe as he released her hand and disappeared.

Crouching beneath the table, she looked after him but saw nothing except blackness.

Footsteps were approaching the laboratory. She heard two voices – the scientists? So close. She stared into the tube falling into the black depths of the ship.

"Ruth!"

Jude's whisper reverberated upwards – close enough for her to hear. Though he was out of sight, his nearness was what she needed. She'd thought he'd slipped away.

Sitting on the floor under the table, she pushed her feet into the vast pipe, forcing apart its taut edges. Her legs dangled free as she edged inside, finding no grip. Then Jude's hands were on her, guiding, helping her. She wriggled the rest of her body inside. The tube closed up above her.

She fell two feet to a flatter level, as though they had dropped down a deck. Inside was suffocating. Disorientating. Sticky. Slippery.

Jude was already crawling away on his hands and knees.

"Get a move on!"

She could barely hear his whisper, sucked away by the vacuum towards the Shadowlands.

She scrabbled around for a grip and found purchase on ridges circling the inside of the pipe, a wind blowing her hair into her eyes. Her cape hood dropped back. There was a sudden glare from her dreamlight.

"Hide it!" Jude whispered urgently, though Ruth was already yanking her hood forwards.

Jude was disappearing into the darkness. She crawled along after him.

Her faintly glowing dream let out a little light around the edges of her hood. She was terrified it would give her away. But the dreamlight reached Jude's worn soles as he crawled rapidly ahead downhill. She made herself concentrate and hurry along after him, working out a faster way to move.

Another spiralling turn downwards.

He reached up and pulled her down after him. Her body, hair, bag, fell into him. The vacuum sucking them towards the Shadowlands was stronger here. He scrambled forwards, leading the way, with a quick glance behind him. Dreamlight shone from beneath Adam's hat, illuminating Jude's eyes, bright in the darkness, framed by his hair, tousled around his face by the strong wind. He smiled quickly and reached for her hand; she felt his thin, quick fingers upon her own. Her heart lifted.

"'Tis the only way we can go." He said the words gently. "We mustn't give up."

He turned and crawled away. She followed the soles of his shoes.

Those shoes . . . Wearing them, he had trodden the streets of Crowbury decades before she'd been born. In them, he'd spoken with Grandfather Richard. He'd addressed the King. And then the dream thieves had come . . . how many *were* there? She and Jude were a million miles from safety. As easily as the shadow-child had slipped down the tube, sucked into the Shadowlands, the dream thieves could shoot along it – whereas she and Jude were made of slow, heavy flesh. They would not stand a chance.

Ruth kept checking over her shoulder as she scrambled along. The snaking blackness behind made her weak with fear.

"*Saboteurs!*"

Faintly they heard the word coming from the laboratory, echoing down the pipe.

"*Stowaways!*"

More shouting followed.

An alarm sounded. It reverberated from beyond the pipe, as though bells were clanging on every deck.

"This'll be the last place they'll think of looking," Jude said.

He slid down the tube as it spiralled lower into the ship. Deeper and lower they moved, twisting and turning, slipping and sliding.

Like the starless darkness of the in-between time she had seen through the portholes, they must now be in some other place. They must have gone beyond the hull – that black sheen she'd seen from Jude's sack as they'd boarded the ship, seething with insects, writhing with limbs. It made no sense. But little did.

The angle dipped sharper and sharper until the ridges could no longer hold them. The force of the wind picked them up and they slipped and fell down, feet first, down and down, faster and faster until the tube disgorged them.

They flew out onto sodden moss.

He pulled her away from the exit of the tube, as she checked her bag and its contents. Both *The Chronicles* and the vial were still intact. Jude stood up and moved away.

She dared not move. Cold, thick air pressed into her skin, crept into her lungs. This place was motionless. Black as pitch. Quiet. Was that the sound of water she could hear running in the distance?

"Jude, where are you?"

She reached out with her hands, for even with the faint light of her dream, she was almost blind in such blackness.

"Stay close," he instructed her, from some way off.

But Ruth remained stock still. There was still a sound like wind – but this time, strangely, no breeze disturbed the hairs on her skin.

"Listen!"

The wind-less rushing, murmuring sounds grew louder.

Ruth felt a rising tide of fear.

These sounds were whispers!

Flat, monotone words, devoid of expression. Some in foreign tongues and some in her own language.

They rose to a crescendo all around her.

She was so afraid she could not help herself from crying out aloud.

"Guardian!"

Just as her words cut through the whispers, her dream emitted a rippling burst of light, a tidal wave of pulsing circles.

The light revealed a low-roofed cave and a seething low mist all around.

Then the hairs on the back of her neck stood up. It wasn't mist but faint figures. Shadow-children!

They surrounded her, their mouths working whispers. Thousands upon thousands. And they were all staring at herself and Jude, shrinking away from the dreamlight.

The whispers fell silent. The ghost-like figures were peering at this spectacle of a real girl and a real boy.

Jude gazed at these shadow-children – whom he had helped to create. He knew this was a consequence of him stealing dreams. He covered his mouth, and bit his fingers. His head swam as his dream pulsed light over the throng.

Above all of them, thin stems of dripping rock dangled from the roof of the cave and glowed in the dreamlight like macabre decorations. Beyond, the roof was out of sight, and in the distance, towering shadows were cast by colossal stone columns which looked like sandstone worn away by rushing water over millennia.

Ruth focused on the souls closest to her. She looked into the dark hollows of their eyes, searching the faces. Was this place a breeding ground for dream thieves? The shadow-children stared back: questioning, despairing, starving. Their expressions spoke of being banished, trapped in this living grave, as though she and Jude were the first living humans they had seen for an eternity.

She glanced at Jude, his eyes round with tears and mouth set hard.

Ruth worried that the shadow-children – abandoned, tortured by despair, dream thieves in the making – would become child soldiers in the dream thieves' army, turn on the pair of them and tear them to pieces. After seeing Sagazan murder the courtier, her mind was full of horrors.

But what actually happened could not have been further from her fears.

A shadow-child close by took the single step required to reach her, and lifted its hand of shadows towards her face. Forcing herself to not lean away, she permitted the faint fingertips to touch her. The child pulled back its hand, as if afraid of warm flesh.

She thought of the blacksmith's boy, then of Little Luce, of Jude himself, of all the children who had been robbed by the dream thieves, of all the children's tears in the Guardian's glass vial. Ruth forced a tentative smile to encourage the shadow-child – though the smile did not stay for long. She was wary. The child lifted his hand once more and Ruth let him stroke her skin, and finger her cheeks and around her eyes.

And then the shadow-child strained higher towards Ruth's dream, just out of reach. He looked her in the eyes, as if in request. Trembling, Ruth lowered her head so that the child could touch the halo. And he did not just touch the dream. He plunged his whole hand into the spinning white light and kept it there while her dream pulsed brighter. Ruth felt the familiar pebble of peace drop inside her.

The next moment was a miracle.

Soft light flowed from her dream down the shadow-child's arm to its body, until the child was covered from head to toe in shimmering dreamlight! The child removed its hand and drifted away, glowing like a firefly.

Ruth could hardly believe her eyes.

More came, stepping forwards and placing their hands in the light of Ruth's dream. She quivered, barely comprehending as each child was filled with dreamlight and stepped away to make room for other shadow-children. They crowded forwards, murmuring with more animation in their voices.

Jude caught her eye and grinned. He was catching the excitement of all this ahead of Ruth; his intuitions in this moment were stronger, for he had just had experienced an extraordinary change of his own. With a flourish, he cast his hat to the floor and his dream shone out.

"Come! Come!" Jude cried out, laughing.

He moved deeper into the crowd, dipping his head so that the shadow-children he had helped to create could reach up and touch his shining halo. Dreamlight was passed onto the little souls. They clustered around him and reached for his dream, which sparkled brighter and brighter the more he bowed his head. He took in the sight of all these shadowchildren, now alight with shimmering brightness from his dream. They were fascinated by the change, staring in amazement at one another.

Watching Jude, Ruth felt witness to something else. She felt a rush of love for this young lad, Master Curiosity, that felt almost brotherly. What would her grandfather make of the pair of them now?

The shadow-children kept pressing in. She continued dipping her head so that they could touch her dream easily.

She thought of the children she knew in Crowbury. It was almost impossible to tell one shadow-child apart from another.

"Little Luce?" She spoke louder, moving amongst the children. "Little Luce?" Some of the nearest watched her lips, hearing her speak, but none responded as though they understood. "Guardian of Dreams," she murmured. "Bring the Crowbury children to me!"

The crowd of shining children turned to the dark souls behind and reached out, touching their heads and hearts – and so the glow spread even further, radiating and rippling outwards, gathering pace until it seemed that thousands of shadow-children were alight with glorious dreamlight. And where was the blacksmith's lad? She didn't know his name and wished that she did. Ruth longed for him to be touched by this flood of light.

Jude was in the distance, reaching the children on the outer edges, the whole cave filled with their silent clamouring for dreamlight.

But at the edge of her awareness was the dark purpose of this underworld.

It would be as solid as the stone that made this cave.

Despair had ruled for so long . . . even the faces of the little ones closest to her seemed to suggest that the hope they were feeling would only last a moment. A frown here, eyes narrowing there, another shadow-child stepping back.

More than that, in a blink, their focus shifted beyond Ruth.

Though still glowing, they drifted away, eyes filling with fear, faces twitching as they stared at a spot behind Ruth's head.

Ruth sensed the intense evil even before she heard the voice.

"Oh, very cosy . . ."

Slowly she turned around.

Sagazan stood there, a blazing black fire in the darkness.

33

Love and Grief

Yellow eyes stared into her own with a mesmerising gaze. Ruth could not move.

"Thinked yer'd got away, did yer? Yer should know this, lickle stowaway. I can smell living dreams." Sagazan lifted the fingers of one hand to his nose, rubbing them delicately together as though sniffing herbs. "They reek. Yer left a stinking easy trail for me to follow. So kind."

"N-not afraid . . . I'm not afraid," Ruth forced the words aloud.

Sagazan smirked and took a step forwards. "Liar." Flames like saliva dripped from his mouth as he pushed his face closer to hers. "We'll see."

Even at this distance she felt a murdering heat, burning through the cold dampness of the Shadowlands. A loose tendril of her hair wavered closer to him and sizzled at the end. The acrid smell of burning filled her nose.

"The Guardian of Dreams is protecting me!"

Sagazan laughed with what seemed like genuine astonishment. "Ha! I thinks not . . . yer tremblin' like a mouse."

"Guardian of Dreams," Ruth desperately repeated the name, her voice wobbling. She took an unsteady step back from this devil as the shadow-children parted behind her. Sagazan followed, never letting her get further than several inches away.

"Guardian, all the way down 'ere? Yer very much mistaken my dear. This 'ere is my realm and these is my children."

He reached out to stroke a shadow-child on the head. His touch drained the glow from the child in an instant. But all the other children were still glowing, and they fixed their eyes on Ruth to see what she would do. It was clear that Sagazan's authority had never been challenged. Until now. Ruth lifted her chin.

"I will never give up on hope!"

Her dreamlight flowed over the surrounding shadow-children.

Sagazan laughed the loudest yet. "That's really very entertainin'!"

Barely moving her head, Ruth searched the sea of glowing shadowy faces for Jude – there he was, deeper into the Shadowlands but closing the distance between them. As he wove through the crowd, his eyes were fixed upon Sagazan.

Sagazan followed her gaze then snapped back to Ruth.

"Zephon would be curious to meet yer, but I'm feelin' inclined to burn yer up 'ere and now. I wouldn't quite kill yer . . . just enough so yer agony'd never end and yer'd join us, 'cos yer'd hate hope too."

"No! I'll never give up on hope!"

"Really? I'll put that to the test." Sagazan opened his jaw as if vomiting up something from his stomach, pursed his lips and blew out a precise jet of fire. She recoiled in terror, her face filled with his fire breath. Her eyelashes singed.

"And, pray, tell me," said the dream thief, "what cause does yer 'av for hope down 'ere?"

"Even here in this hell you've made, my dream is still working," Ruth said, lifting her chin again. "It still shines, and I think that scares you."

Sagazan stopped moving and collected himself. "Does I look scared?!"

She gestured to those around her. "You've never seen these children like this before. They're less under your control than you think."

Sagazan snarled.

The shadow-children were looking frantically from Ruth to Sagazan and back again. She felt coolness touch her palm. Glancing down, a child had slipped her hand into her own. A sudden force of conviction washed over Ruth. The war waged against dreams by these evil creatures would *not* be won so easily.

Ruth eyeballed Sagazan, gathering all the strength she could muster. "You cannot see," Ruth continued, "that your own perverted dream is to rid the world of all dreams, every last one, and if you destroy *all* dreams you will destroy yourself!"

While she spoke, Sagazan narrowed his eyes and rippled his muscles, fury building. It gave her courage. Surely he was angry because she was speaking the truth.

"That so?" Sagazan snarled. "Your lil' friend is awful quiet. He don't seem to agree."

The dream thief turned to Jude, just a stride away.

He was speechless though his dream was spinning white. This girl, this brave girl, seconds away from death, still fighting, clinging on to hope!

To Ruth, Jude's expression was impossible to read. All she knew was that, even in the strange light cast by the ethereal shadow-children and his dream, his cheeks were drained of colour. Sagazan cocked his head to one side and looked the boy up and down.

"Yes, lad . . . yer dream's reekin' too. Come 'ere."

Sagazan snapped his fingers and pointed at the floor of the cave before him. Jude stepped forwards to the spot. Slowly he lifted his eyes to Sagazan's towering presence.

"She's the stowaway, but what about you?" Sagazan's low tone made his voice all the more threatening.

No words came out of Jude's mouth.

"Turncoat?" Sagazan growled. "No?"

Jude stared at Sagazan with a look of universal knowledge. He had seen it all. He knew the worst of it all. He had been enslaved to the hell of the dream thieves. And now, perhaps in some tiny way, he had redeemed himself, restoring a little hope to some of these lost souls he must have helped to create.

"Ah. I sees it." Sagazan read him correctly. "And yer shiny new dream." Sagazan clenched and unclenched his fists and cast a glance at Ruth. His chest puffed out. He addressed the shadow-children around Jude. "This lad won't save yer – stole yer dreams in the first place. Made yer cry."

Shadow-children were drifting away from Jude. Ruth thought of the vial of tears in her bag. The tears it contained might have fallen from their eyes as real children. Her hand almost reached for the vial, as if in comfort.

"I thought . . ." Jude said, "p'raps I was doing good."

Ruth stared at him. Was he talking about his thieving – or what had just taken place? Was he excusing himself to the shadow-children or to Sagazan?

Sagazan seemed to grow in stature, rearing up.

Jude's spinning dream stuttered. The light flared. Was it faltering? Ruth knew she should take this chance to get further away. But she couldn't tear her eyes from Jude's dream. She backed up, her hands reaching out behind, her feet slipping on the rocks, her eyes not leaving the two of them for one moment. Quietly, desperately, she called on the Guardian.

"Yer was a good lickle magpie, collecting the brightest dreams of the lot. Yer back in the fold now, ain't yer . . . 'cos if yer aint, I'll make yer worse than dead." Sagazan whirled towards Ruth. "Going somewhere?"

Sagazan breathed out taunting black flames. His focus shifted to Ruth's spinning white dream, but it refused to falter. He snarled and came after her, reaching out to grab it.

"DON"T YOU TOUCH HER!" Jude's rage was heard through the Shadowlands, his eyes blazing.

It was enough for Sagazan to hesitate for a moment – and for Ruth to run – but where to?

What happened next, Ruth could never have foreseen.

Jude lunged at Sagazan, going for his throat. Sagazan arced away, all blazing flame, and Jude thumped to the ground. Sagazan scowled at Ruth, making to come at her again, as Jude scrambled to his feet and charged at the dream thief, aiming his head low and headbutting Sagazan in the chest. But Sagazan stood firm, his rear foot gripping the ground.

Jude was trying to protect her!

"Run, Ruth! Run!" Jude threw her a glance, courage shining in his eyes as he flung himself at Sagazan once more.

"No!!!" she cried out. Jude wouldn't stand a chance. She couldn't lose him! She was frozen to the spot as Sagazan toyed with her friend. The dream thief dodged away from Jude's fists, laughing.

The shadow-children melted away from the fight into the further reaches of the cave. Shaking with fear, Ruth took one step backwards, calling once again for the Guardian.

Sagazan circled Jude, flames of saliva dripping. His fire breath met Jude at full force, torching Jude from head to toe. Clothes, hair, flesh, all exploded screaming in an inferno.

She could bear to look no longer, hiding her eyes behind her arm, but she could not shield herself from his agonised screams. They rang out around the Shadowlands, stabbing her heart.

Jude had sacrificed himself.

Sagazan would come for her next.

A sudden movement behind her. A strong breeze at her back. Her eyes brimming, she turned. What new foe was this?

A blur of black feathers, barely visible through her tears. Muscular arms. Coils of black hair . . . lit by a spinning white dream! His face full of great alarm.

She let out a sob. Godrick!

34

Last Gasp

At once, hundreds of multi-coloured winged messengers landed on the ground with soft thuds amongst all the shadow-children, filling the cave with the sudden brightness of their dream light.

Sagazan recoiled, lifting his hands to shield his black eyes. A pile of ash was falling where Jude had just stood. Like black snow. It transfixed her, the horror sinking deep.

She felt Godrick's hand on her shoulder as he swiftly searched the darkness beyond her. Ruth knew the messengers could not see Sagazan, just as Adam could not see Jude. They were blind to the evil. But surely they would feel it!

"Climb onto my back, Ruth," Godrick urged, stepping forwards and bending down on one knee, revealing the four joints through his robe where his wings met his spine. "Do it now!"

"The shadow-children!" she cried, with one hand on his back.

"We will make them safe. Climb up!"

Ruth used the wing joints as footholds, scrambling up as Godrick's inner wings folded around her, protecting her. And just in time.

Sagazan had recovered, but as he lunged at Godrick with his black flame fingers, he was cut down to the ground by the immense power of Godrick's dream.

All around them, the other messengers were enfolding the glowing children in their wings, too. The children clung to the ones they hoped would rescue them.

But their escape was not to be that easy.

Horrific screeching suddenly filled the cave as dream thieves poured out of the dark mouth of the pipe and into the Shadowlands, flying, running and swooping towards Ruth and the messengers with deafening shrieks.

Carrying the glowing children, with one beat of their wings, the messengers simply disappeared in little puffs of light, leaving the dream thieves in their wake. Sagazan's minions grasped at the empty air, searching for the vanished shadow-children.

Sagazan was enraged, becoming all fire.

Godrick extended his wings to fly away but Sagazan spat out long black flames that scorched his magnificent feathers. Godrick screamed and flinched, casting around for his invisible attacker.

Desperate, Ruth fumbled in her bag with one hand while keeping herself upright on Godrick's back. She was searching for the vial of tears.

Sagazan, with a terrible grimace, lunged forwards with his black flames to attack. But Ruth pulled out the glass vial from her bag. She yanked out the stopper and with as strong a throw as she could muster, emptied the bottle, throwing the tears into the air. It was the only thing she could do.

Droplets cascaded through the Shadowlands, glittering in the light of their dreams until they showered down upon Sagazan.

Sagazan clutched his eyes and stumbled, disorientated, to the ground. Ruth gasped.

He staggered, blinded by the intense purity of the tears. He screamed powerfully and it echoed around the walls of his domain.

Hearing it, the mass of dream thieves turned towards Ruth and Godrick and raced towards them, screeching a battle cry. But the tears from the vial took on a life of their own and multiplied until there were as many as the stars – a vast wave of crystal drops refracting light as thousands of tiny rainbows – and they clashed with the dream thieves like armies on a battlefield. The tears were the instant victors. Within two heartbeats the dream thieves were screaming and clutching their sizzling eyes.

"NOW! Godrick we must leave NOW," Ruth shouted above the horrific noise, crouching deep into his feathers to shield herself.

But Godrick, sensing the army of evil and not knowing they had been blinded, stumbled backwards. As he lost his balance, he opened his wings.

Eyes wide with terror, Ruth desperately tried to hold on as Godrick fell to one side. Her fingers slid through his feathers. Her feet slipped down his back. Her cape caught on a wing, pulling the collar tighter and tighter around her neck, choking her. Godrick moved forwards, unwittingly increasing the tension. She was being strangled by her own cape. Her fingers tore at her neck. Her feet were sliding down the robe over his legs. The cape squeezed her neck tighter, tighter. She couldn't breathe! And then the fastener broke, releasing her in one tumble to the ground, her hands thumping against bare rock, jarring her shoulders and neck.

Screaming and screeching was filling the air – the dream thieves, demented with anger and the agony of their blindness. She scrambled backwards, further away. Godrick had fallen forwards and was turning back towards her. But suddenly her hands slipped into nothingness and she found herself falling backwards through the air – falling, falling – till her body hit icy wetness, sinking into unending water!

The underground river folded around her, instantly cutting off all sound, all air, seeping into the curves of her body, her eyes and ears and mouth, every strand of hair, as an undercurrent pulled her down and down, deeper and deeper into the dark water. She reached up in vain towards the air of the Shadowlands but there was nothing she could do to stop the relentless pull of the current. She grasped for a hold, seeing her white bony fingers reaching out, but sharp rocks lacerated her fingertips releasing little blooms of red blood in the water, and still the current pulled her along and down, bubbles of air cascading out of her mouth and nose.

She struggled. Frantic. Fighting for life.

The stream twisted and shot beneath rocks. She bobbed up for one moment in a tiny cavern, the roof just inches above her head. She gasped in the pocket of air, coughing and choking, before the force of the current dragged her under again. Images of her friend swirled into view, dearest Jude, dying, every square inch of his body burning to dust. Still tumbling through water, her limbs felt leaden, battered numb and weak with cold, and soon she felt nothing but a seductive sleepiness, a profound exhaustion that beckoned her to drift away into a new place, a softer place, away from evil, to let go . . .

The stream carried her body further underground, slowing its pace as the water took almost the last air from her lungs, and she knew she was drowning. All around her, on the sparkling crystals on rocks, she saw faint images . . . all those she loved and cared for . . . mother's face, father . . . her half-sister . . . Little Luce . . . Nurse . . . Silas . . . Silas . . . pictures from her life in Crowbury, all glittering on the crystals, and she was too numb with cold to feel her heart break with loss as the last of the air in her lungs was used up and her dream dimmed and darkness closed around her.

35

Moonbow

Ruth opened her eyes. She was shuddering with cold, but she could breathe. She could breathe! Coughing up water, she took great gulps of air. She came to, trying to focus. Her dream was spinning and reflecting on pearls of water, coating . . . glossy dark feathers? A messenger? Godrick? Her fingers traced over taut plumage that could only be wings. Sounds came from beyond: rushing water. Was that the underground river – was she safe in this pocket of air? Was she held by closed wings?

Ruth shuddered, waiting to see what would happen next. The sound of water receded and the feathers around her opened into wings, revealing in an instant the roof of a huge cavern. She gasped and clung to the messenger's shoulders as she lay on his back. Was this the Shadowlands again? But moonlight was there, up ahead. It was pouring through an opening towards which the messenger was speeding with all his might, outer wings beating strongly as his inner wings held her in place. Heart racing, eyes darting, she looked for dream thieves and shadow-children. There was only dark, damp rock and the surging river in which she had almost drowned.

"'Tis you?" Her words came out in a whisper.

She heard Godrick's deep voice reply. "Yes . . . Hush now . . ."

In two great wingbeats they were out of the cave, soaring into the starlit night, flying hundreds of feet into the air. His head turned this way and that, determining which way to go. Or was he looking out for dream thieves? She scrutinised the sky for a dark hole that could be the ship hunting them down. But there was just starlight.

" . . . I . . ."

The broken, dead dreams . . . the horror of Jude burning to dust . . . all she had witnessed . . . every moment was imprinted on her mind and body. She could not put any words together and make her mouth work.

"Rest now, Ruth. We will have time enough to talk. Soon."

The moon shone, so full, bright, steady, drawing them closer. She fixed her eyes on it, hoping its white brightness would blot out the dark horrors she felt inside. Her Armillary Sphere came to mind, its crystal Moon sparkling in candlelight. And now she pictured the perverted version of it on the ship, its blazing Sun in the centre, empowering the dream thieves to wreak their evil . . . She screwed up her eyes and opened them, focusing on the moon-lit coils of Godrick's hair and the red and green tones of his raven-like wings which swept through the night sky.

Slowly, the terror of the Shadowlands faded with every mile that put a greater distance between Ruth and the dream thieves. Little by little, her limbs softened and relaxed. Her sodden, ragged nightgown gradually dried out in the night air and with the warmth of Godrick's body. Living, breathing. Wings and feathers. His goodness. His safe presence.

The words he had spoken in her bedchamber had driven every decision she had made since they first met. *Hold fast to your dreams*, he had said, echoing her own father. The words had taken on a visceral meaning. Never could she have imagined the consequences: Jude's transformation and sacrifice . . . and where had the messengers taken the shadow-children? She shifted on his back, suddenly restless.

"I can take you home, Ruth," Godrick said, with a glance over his shoulder.

Home.

The word shot through her. Bright. Burning. She had given up on ever seeing Crowbury Hall again. All she knew was that even with the Countess, it was a thousand times better than the dream thief's ship, or being lost in some other place and time.

Home.

Knowing where she was headed, she succumbed to the exhaustion she had been fighting. Through half-open eyes she saw the night sky glittering with pinprick stars and mountains stretching far away, folded like fabric, creases in the Earth. Streams criss-crossed and joined forces, swelling into rivers like streaks of silver across the landscape. But she could not sleep, and did not want to; she was savouring the miracle of being alive. Wind kissed her face and flew through her hair. Every breath felt like her first. She lifted her hand, cupped it around her mouth, feeling the warmth each time she exhaled. These were blissful things, and she noticed them all at the same time as the images of deathly horrors that still ran through her mind.

On and on they flew as the moon crept across the sky. Stars wheeled and turned. Godrick changed direction and tipped gently downwards. The mountain range was petering out. Treetops were just beneath now. Beech and pine and oak as she had never seen them before, lush green branches radiating outwards from the trunks. Flying between the trees was an owl. It looked up at the strange fliers, its huge eyes meeting hers, then turned back to searching for prey.

There was a new sound.

Ruth heard the tremendous thundering of the waterfall before she saw it.

"Ah, there it is," Godrick said, more to himself than to her, as he dived down towards it.

Sheets of water cascaded hundreds of feet to a boiling river below, falling so fast it made Ruth dizzy. A giant bow of pale colours caught her eye – the echo of a rainbow at night. A moonbow!!! Her heart leapt. She had read of such things in a book of natural wonders. It arced high above the waterfall, shimmering in the billowing misty spray, gleaming in the moonlight. So rare, so beautiful, it beckoned her. And Godrick was making straight for it.

They plunged into the colours so that the hairs on her skin lifted and her whole body tingled.

They flew deeper inside as she gazed around. This strange, ethereal bow seemed to have no end – yet still the riverside and forest were visible through the iridescent colours. Awestruck, she looked closer at the stripes of colour . . . there were dreams! Hundreds of halos hovering mid-air. There was something else, too. While the waterfall roared beneath, inside the shelter of the moonbow all was remarkably hushed . . . but there *was* a sound. She listened closer. Children's voices, rising and falling in song. There were many different tongues singing in harmony – the exact opposite of the bleak whisperings in the Shadowlands. But these voices were joyful, not despairing . . .

Suddenly before her eyes was a vision of thousands of glowing shadow-children. Not in the Shadowlands, but tumbling out of flurries of multi-coloured feathers onto long grasses in a dew-drenched forest, as a host of messengers released them. It was the forest she had seen before, with fruit-laden trees and the bubbling spring. She focused on the vision more closely. Some of the shadow-children were gathering around the Guardian of Dreams, bright shining, the crown of light blazing. Others reached out for one another, and still more gazed at the messengers who responded, drawing close to the children.

The Guardian smiled and held out an arm to embrace the nearest shadow-child, turning to look into the deep dark pool that bubbled up from the ground. Water droplets ascended. The Guardian lifted fingers to orchestrate a misty image of a real child and a dream halo that from the water to encircle its head. The Guardian guided this misty child with its dream halo downwards to the grassy bank where it joined the glowing shadow-child . . . not just joined, but reconciled . . . a child made whole. The child disappeared. Ruth gasped. As the Guardian took the hand of the next shadow-child, the scene faded from her sight. And what came back into focus was the moonbow, and all the hovering dreams still enveloping her. Children's voices were still singing.

Dizzy and dazed, she put her hand to her head. Then she felt Godrick's hand firm upon her shoulder, calling her back to this moment in the moonbow. Dreams glistened around them, and he looked right into the core of her.

"We were drawn to the dreamlight. It was shining out from where you were with all those lost souls. Can you tell us what took place, Ruth?"

Words rose up. At first Ruth stumbled over her speech, as though just even reporting on such evil might poison her lips or evoke a dream thief. And as she spoke with increasing urgency, the dreams shimmered around her like living things . . . so many she couldn't take it in . . . Jade green faded to yellow ochre, pumpkin merged into red with the delicacy of grapeskin deepening into amber, then chestnut brown darkening to grey, then lightening into the colours of lavender and amethyst crystal and the intense blue of sea and sky. The halos muffled her torrent of words about the dream thieves, and Jude's terrible death, so that not a word escaped the moonbow and touched the world around them . . . not one fish flicking its silver tail in the tumbling river, nor the mouse creeping through the field nor the owl circling above it that felt the air tremble. Every word she said was held by

Godrick and the dreams around them. She was sure, now, that this unearthly moonbow was a gateway to another place. And she was sure that the Guardian of Dreams was listening, too.

Godrick was pensive, looking down at his lightly folded hands, taking in all that she had shared.

Her hands at her side, she became aware of the dripping weight still around her body. The hunting bag! She lifted the flap. *The Chronicles* were there, but as she pulled out the book, water dripped. They were drenched from the Shadowlands' underground river! All the pages were running with streaks of ink. Nothing was discernible. No dust cloud appeared, no Adam.

She felt undone, lost. She closed her eyes, almost fainting . . .

36

A Declaration

She stood alone at the foot of her bed, blinking, her toes gripping oak floorboards, her knees bent and arms outstretched for balance. Her skin glistened with a fine mist, warmed by steady sunshine that was falling through her window. Drops of water were falling. They came from the drenched, ruined *Chronicle of Dreams* in her hand. Looped over her body was the hunting bag. Her nightgown was damp from the moonbow. She reached for the bedpost to steady herself, and winced – her palms were red raw. Her eyes lifted, fixing on the rainbow carved into her bedhead. She breathed deeply. Her head was full of the glowing shadow-children in the flower-strewn grass with the Guardian of Dreams.

Her bed was unmade, her feather pillows still creased and dented from where her head had rested. Her things were just as she had left them. Yesterday's dress on a chair. Boots on the floor. An open book of poetry on the table: *The Faerie Queene*.

Outside, bare branches were swaying in a breeze.

Noises reached her from the Hall. Muffled voices, doors closing, footsteps, a shout, laughter. The family was back. Smells were drifting up from the kitchen . . . roasting meat, fresh warm milk and herbs. She breathed deeply again and sat exhausted on the end of her bed, holding *The Chronicles*. And she knew what she had to do.

★   ★   ★

The clock outside her bedchamber struck midday. Ruth closed her door. She had put on her best gown, pinned her hair up in a bun, laced up her feet in ankle boots and fixed a fresh cape around her neck, pulling it over the bruises from the Shadowlands. *The Chronicles* were safely hidden away in the secret place behind her bed; she would look at it later, feel its pages under her touch.

She was still standing beside the clock, and blinked slowly. She needed to face the Countess, back from Little Appleton, and Lord Boswell, her supposed betrothed – if he had already arrived. And then, whatever happened, she would go to Crowbury church, see what had become of the fallen roof and draw strength in the quietness by her mother's tomb, thinking of Jude and all that had taken place.

The winter sun glowed through the glass in the corridor. She paused, her hand on the window, looking down at the courtyard. A coach was there, the horses already uncoupled and presumably put away in the stables.

Footsteps. It was Nurse . . . her warm brown eyes, bobbing curls and pink cheeks. Ruth grabbed her and hugged her tight. Nurse patted Ruth on the back and took a little step backwards, her eyebrows raised at the sudden affection.

"Dearie me, well yes, that man *has* arrived," Nurse said, with a nod to the coach below. "I was coming to find you."

Nurse evidently thought the warmth of Ruth's greeting was because she was still scared of Lord Boswell. Little did she know.

But, yes, the man had come to seal the arrangement and claim his bride.

"I will go to them, and then I will need some air," Ruth said, touching her cape.

"She hasn't called for you yet, but I don't suppose it will be long."

Nurse pressed her lips together, and glanced behind herself and beyond Ruth, checking for the presence of others. Her voice fell into a whisper.

"I weren't sure when to give you this, but I think it's best to do it now, before, well . . ." She hastily pulled a note from her pocket and offered it to Ruth. "Silas said to give you this. He's gone and left Crowbury."

Silas. She had almost forgotten about him, yet her heart still slipped a beat. She was too surprised to find any words. The note was crumpled and sweaty. She felt the sting of his betrayal for one moment, and in the next knew that if her heart was truly broken, it was over the death of Jude, not the loss of Silas. It was Jude who gave his all – not like Silas, who was so far from the person she'd thought he was. Silas, her childhood friend, her first love, had only put himself first – even if he said it was all for his family's sake. But she would not be too harsh, for this may have been the work of the dream thieves.

All she knew was that Silas felt like a foreign land to her now. Her heart had cooled.

Nurse clicked her tongue. "I know you was very fond of him, and he of you. He left yesterday afternoon, after you two . . . well he's gone to London." With a squeeze of her arm, Nurse left.

And to think, Ruth had almost pitched her life on him. She unfurled the note. The sight of his inky strokes made her feel a little sick. She retreated to her room and walked back and forth as she read it.

It was an apology, simply put. At least he was man enough to give her that. The note was addressed to no-one and signed by no-one: to protect her – or him. She trusted he was away to find a bookbinder who would take him on, and hoped he would pursue what he wanted to do. But as for their love, it was in the past.

The girl she was yesterday felt so far away.

Ruth crushed the note into a ball and threw it into the grate where it caught fire. Orange flames sprang up as it shrank and fell apart. A memory of Sagazan flickered there. Once again, she left and made for the stairs.

Voices drifted towards her. The Countess.

The door to the Withdrawing Room was open an inch. Ruth slowed her step. The woman's voice became clear, low and silky. Then a man's voice she did not recognise. Boswell. It sickened her. Their conversation fell quiet.

She pushed on the door and stopped in her tracks.

The Countess was sitting in her usual spot beside the fireplace, obscured by the figure of Boswell, who was bending down, his lips to the Countess's neck! Ruth's mouth gaped open. The two of them were oblivious to her presence. Boswell continued to plant kisses on the Countess's skin. And then they both saw her. Boswell stood upright, his bearded lips apart revealing crooked teeth, his hooded eyes stretching wide open. He put one hand in a pocket. The Countess was gripping the arms of the chair, her expression unfathomable.

Ruth stood where she was and held their eyes, held the silence. Her stomach twisted. Her voice steady, she declared her resolution, her words hanging in the air. She looked from one to the other, and as there was no reply, calmly walked out.

I do not consent. Her words rang in her ears as she passed Boswell's coach in the courtyard. She stepped over the remains of the snow and the deep grooves cut by his wheel rims in the wet gravel, heading for the gateway. At the sound of a barking dog, she glanced back. Bess ran out of the stables – pursued by Little Luce.

Little Luce!

Hair flying, feet skidding, dancing around Bess. The dog barked and jumped up as she teased him with a stick held high – seeing Ruth, she grinned and waved it in the air like a flag. Without realising it, Ruth put one hand to her heart. She waved back, and nodding to herself, continued on her way.

Ruth touched the stone crest on her family's gateway as she rounded the corner onto the track down through the wood. She skipped over the churned up mud, heading in the opposite direction from which Boswell had come. She thought of the multitude of journeys the track had witnessed down through the years – everyone she had ever known had passed this way, and before that her ancestors, and King Henry . . . even Jude with his candles. She sighed and looked up. Beyond the branches, the great blue sky deepened as the sun bowed out on the day, casting clouds in pink.

I do not consent.

Ruth patted each trunk as she passed by, feeling the bark. The trees stood as if in sturdy solidarity with her, their roots sunk deep into her life. These trees held treasured moments with her mother. They held whispered secrets with Silas. All had passed and gone, but still the trees stood.

I do not consent.

Damp lichen curled in the cooling air. The last of the ice was melting. Her foot struck a puddle. Relishing the mud seeping into the soles, she laughed and pulled her boots off, feeling the freezing wet earth squelch between her toes. All around, the winter mulch gave off a smell like iron which penetrated deep into her lungs with every breath. She pulled her hair out of the bun and shook her curls loose.

She was alive.

And she would never be betrothed to Boswell.

For witnessing their unlawful intimacy, Ruth would be hated even more. But she did not care. In being seen, the pair of them had unmade the future they had contrived. The unyielding Countess had undone herself. They had sabotaged their own dark dreams.

Coming round the bend, Ruth could see Crowbury church through the trees, the roof still open to the sky. She would go and sit beside her mother's tomb and touch once again the rainbow carved in stone. She stepped onwards down the lane, dangling her boots by the laces and hitching her skirt above the mulch. Her ankles were pink in the cold, and her feet would be too, if they were not covered in mud.

Something had taken place in the moonbow that had eased her soul. It had lifted part of the burden of all she had seen and felt, yet some remained. Perhaps she could fold it away, keep it secret, like *The Chronicles* and those books hidden behind her bed. Though, even if she could hide what had taken place from others, she could never hide it from herself. Fear crept out. Then she called to mind the beautiful thing she had glimpsed just minutes before, Little Luce and Bess.

The church was there. Reaching the graveyard, she paused, her hand on the gate. A robin danced and sang along the wall.

She stepped down the pathway towards the porch. Wind caught her hair and it blew across her eyes as she became dimly aware of galloping hooves behind her and the clatter of a coach along the track. She gathered her hair to one side, pulling it out of her eyes. There was a shout. Ruth turned. A fist thumped urgently against wood. The coach screeched to an abrupt halt.

The brown-gloved hand that reached out through the open window to release the door handle was familiar. As was the shape of the leg and navy breeches, and the way the man, nimble for his age, jumped down from the coach. Through her sudden tears, she saw a delighted grin fill his face as his eyes met hers. He swung around the gate and ran down the path towards her. Ruth had longed beyond longing for his return. And here he was.

Perhaps . . . surely . . . he had dreamt of coming home.

She cried out to him. "Father!"

Acknowledgements

Ever since it first came to me, the story of Ruth and the Guardian of Dreams gripped me and would not let me go. I started other novels but always felt pulled back to this, until it finally found its true north. First draft to publication took twelve years. Along the way, I was a single mum working full time, writing in the margins of the day. It was a journey, to say the least, and there are many people I want to thank.

Firstly, my agent Lindsey Fraser. Thank you for your endless encouragement and words of wisdom. Your idea to use Silas's point of view was the catalyst for the final breakthrough. I want to thank my publisher, Jean Findlay at Scotland Street Press, for giving *Black Snow Falling* its home, and David Robinson for seeing those 'milliseconds of doubt' in his copy edits.

Thanks to Karen Moran, the Librarian at the Royal Observatory in Edinburgh, for allowing me to handle an original copy of Copernicus's *On the Revolution of The Heavenly Orbs*. It had been there all along, just a mile up the hill from where I'd been writing about it. I'm grateful to the London Science Museum for their old Optical Department, which inspired the Optical Figuring machine – forgive me for bending physics. The National Library of Scotland for the 16th century books that sparked the idea for *The Chronicles of Dreams*. The Museo Galileo in Florence for the mechanical Medici Armillary Sphere, made in the 1500s. It was so extraordinary, it lodged itself in the cogs of my mind long before the idea for this novel came together. And for that, I am indebted to the young adults I met while volunteering for Venture Scotland at a remote bothy in Glen Etive. While we hiked back to the van, one told me that he wanted to get out of the city and work in the forests or become a gardener. Despite the many painful challenges he'd clearly faced, he still had hope. I found myself wanting nothing worse to happen that could snatch his hopes away . . . a chilling *'what if?'* started to haunt me. During the long drive back to Edinburgh, the manager, Fiona, mentioned that Glen Etive, with countless waterfalls cascading down the mountains, had been described as a "land of rainbows" by Wordsworth . . . and the idea for this novel started to come together.

Tim Byrne, thank you for the beautiful, subtle and creepy cover that captures the atmosphere of the novel. I'd always hoped that one day it would be you who designed the cover because I knew you'd nail it – it was, and you did.

I want to thank the author Nicola Morgan for sharpening my writing after the first draft. Anna and fellow writers at SCBWI. Kamala, for the name of Silas. Gill, for letting me use the phenomenon in the night. Helen, for sharing early dreams. Claire, for always helping me to see the thread. And the rest of my friends – you know who you all are – for mutual courage, laughter and glasses of wine. Especially Andy and Jude and Stephen, for companionship in the call of creativity and feeling completely nuts.

My sisters Katy and Gilly, for times spent running around the grounds of Bramall Hall – which became Crowbury Hall.

Rupert, finding me at the eleventh hour with your soul-mate love. Thank you for your poetic eye, the fallen roof and our golden yarn.

Acknowledgements

Jenny, with your beautiful, free heart . . . Thanks for putting up with a distracted writing mum over so many years on our adventure together.

My parents, to whom I am LJ, I owe everything. Words can never say enough, Mum . . . and dear Dad in the ether.

www.ljmacwhirter.com

10% of the author's net income from the sale of this book will be donated to Venture Scotland to help disadvantaged young people swim against the stream.